HARVEST OF A GOLDEN SKY

HARVEST
OF A
GOLDEN
SKY

RICHARD F. SUGG

Matador
Unit E2 Airfield Business Park,
Harrison Road, Market Harborough,
Leicestershire. LE16 7UL
Tel: 0116 2792299
Email: books@troubador.co.uk
Web: www.troubador.co.uk/matador
Twitter: @matadorbooks

ISBN 978 1803135 700

British Library Cataloguing in Publication Data.
A catalogue record for this book is available from the British Library.

Printed and bound in Great Britain by CMP UK
Typeset in 11pt Minion Pro by Troubador Publishing Ltd, Leicester, UK

Matador is an imprint of Troubador Publishing Ltd

For my Wife and Family

ONE

The tall rooster tail of hot desert dust tracked the well-worn pick-up as it sped along the burning desert road. At the wheel was an average-looking guy concentrating on the job in hand; eyes firmly fixed on the open straight horizon and counting off the miles as small but familiar landmarks appeared and then receded in the dust. The sweat salt-stained baseball cap and aviator specs defied the rush of dusty warm air that curled past the windscreen pillar. His chin sported a day's growth of stubble, but the night and day had been long, and life for Ven Carlson was all about priorities and right now, getting to Desert Field by four in the afternoon was what life was all about. There was no logical explanation for this self-imposed target; it was just a reasonable time he had fixed in his own mind twenty-four hours ago, and Ven hated to be beaten by anything... worthwhile or not!

1

Cresting over the next ridge brought Desert Field clearly into view; he had made it with four minutes to spare. Taking his foot off the gas pedal, he allowed the old V8 to regain her composure. Strange, he thought, how he always referred to engines, motors and aeroplanes as females but comforted himself in the fact that most of his friends did exactly the same. Seconds later, he was shaken out of his contentment by the banshee shriek of a Packard-built Rolls-Royce Merlin as it hauled a P-51D Mustang up into a perfect loop way above his head. Such a sight was no big deal for Ven. For a long time now, this superb old aeroplane had been a dominant part of his life. His late father could take responsibility for that. He pulled over, jumped out and, half leaning on the old Chevy, simply indulged himself in the pleasure of what was happening in the big clear blue sky above him. Pulling the cap firmly over his eyes and squinting into the sun, he muttered quietly to himself, "Pretty flying, Mr Smith, but not quite there… just yet!"

The Mustang headed west flat and fast and then curved back towards the airfield, flashed along the runway at about 400 feet and completed the run with a break, hauling into a left-hand circuit and neatly bleeding off speed for altitude, the landing gear coming down before she settled into a near-perfect curved approach. Ven watched as it dropped out of view behind some airfield buildings but was reassured by the sound of the popping Merlin as the Mustang, now firmly back on the ground, started to slow, indicating all was well. Relaxed, he clambered back into the truck; why all the concern? Well, this aluminium lady was his, and she had been for many… many years now, the focal point of his life, his everything. There were those about him who doubted his sanity, and even one concerned friend who had half-jokingly offered the address of his shrink. Ven Carlson wasn't a man who cared much for the opinions of others. His father had given him plenty of advice, some good, some bad but, *Sometimes son there is no pleasing everyone and if that happens, you just got to please yourself,* still worked for him.

Passing through the gate, he acknowledged the wave and cheery call of the gateman and made for the flight line to greet Rusty Smith, his partner, who would have been flying the Mustang. With the sun glinting off the canopy, the WW2 fighter weaved its way back from the far end of the field. Ven thought about a cigarette but resisted the temptation. "Two weeks now, not bad!"

A hand slapped him on the back. "Ven, you son of a moose, how the hell are you? Did you manage to get those carburettor parts?"

Ven wheeled around, shocked and angry. "Rusty, what the fuck is going on here? I thought that was you! Who in hell's name is in the *Angel*? And you'd better be ready to do some fast talking."

"For Christ's sake, calm down, man. It's a customer and pretty good at that."

"Well, I can see it's not one of the regulars. Who is it and why… why didn't you call me?"

"Steady on, old friend. I am supposed to be your partner, remember. This was a good business deal. We had a five-day cancellation and this came out of the blue. It was just too good to miss."

"OK, fine, but just tell me straight. You weren't looking through the bottom of a glass when you made this deal, were you?"

Rusty stepped back, genuinely angered and hurt by his old friend's comments.

"You ungrateful bastard. That's pretty much below the belt, even from you." He paused, collected himself, turned away but swung back. "This one is good, very good, maybe one day as good as you. Just keep your mouth shut for five minutes and look and listen for a change!"

The Mustang came to rest in front of them and a mechanic placed two wooden chocks under the wheels.

The two partners watched as the black-helmeted pilot, now clearly visible through the slid-back canopy, completed the post-flight checks.

"Flash headgear!" Rusty did not rise to the bait. Ven was now cooling, just like the Merlin, but whilst he was still slightly annoyed that this 'stranger' could handle his ship so well, he was intrigued as to whom it might be. There weren't too many flyers around who could handle the *Angel* as well as him; he was proud but not too proud to learn from the very best.

The slim dark flight-suited figure exited the cockpit, slid down the wing and athletically jumped onto the tarmac before walking the 50 yards towards them.

"Christ, it's just a kid."

"Shut up."

"Aren't we taking some chances here, Rusty?" The anger was beginning to well up again. "Let's hope the Feds don't get to hear about this."

"Calm down, Ven. Believe me, it's no kid, mid-thirties, owner of 5,000 hours on heavies, not to mention plenty of time on Yaks and Extras."

"OK, OK, I can handle it… I always do when you drop

me in it." The black-suited figure stood in front of them and removed its helmet. Rusty closed his eyes and waited.

"You must be Ven Carlson... pleased to meet you."

Ven stood still and then, with more surprise than anger, slowly mouthed, "Oh no... a Limey, and not only that... a woman, for God's sake."

"Well, full marks for observation, but I think you have broken a whole hatful of PC values there, Mr Carlson." Rusty interjected to try and save the situation.

"Take no account of his manners, miss. He wouldn't know a PC value if it stood right up and bit him. All he cares about is this pile of aluminium and steel he calls the *Angel*."

Ven nodded apologetically and Rusty started breathing normally again.

"OK, come on over to the flight office and we can talk about things over a cup of coffee."

They walked in silence with Ven, now very angry with himself, asking himself the question, *Why do I never think before I open my big mouth?*

Over coffee, Kirsten Davies explained that she was indeed an airline command pilot on Boeing 737s. Her spare-time passion was competition aerobatics and, not only that: she was a qualified flying instructor as well.

This visit, she explained, was the fulfilment of a life-long dream. She had contacted the 'ANGEL MUSTANG COMPANY', and, having been lucky enough to get this one-week cancellation slot, had thrown herself into the task with the same passion and professionalism she had given to all her flying.

"I started here on Monday first thing and Rusty has put me through all the hoops, including three hours' dual and a tech exam, the full works. Believe me, this is something I knew I wanted and must do. The aeroplane fits like a glove, a second skin. Everything I have done here has been easy, almost as if I have done it before."

"Well, that's fine," interjected Ven, with the emphasis on the FINE, still not comfortable with the situation. "And what has Wonder Boy here fixed up for you tomorrow? Are we going to fly through the hangar inverted?"

Rusty winced but Kirsten caught the funny side of the comment. Ven's jealous passion over the *Angel* was nothing new; Rusty had been dealing with minor outbursts like this for many years.

"Well, I thought that Miss Davies here might like an introduction to some formation aerobatics. She has plenty of formation aero experience on Yak 52s."

Ven was jumping in again headfirst. "Now hold on here, we have never gone from rank beginner to formation aeros in one week before. Who does she think she is? Ed Shipley or something?"

"Now, Mr Carlson, that would be difficult seeing as I am a woman."

Ven's face creased into a smile and he nodded in silent agreement.

"OK, sorry... I will go along with it... as long as all the paperwork and reports are in order. Oh, and just one other thing – I'll be flying the other Mustang!"

*

The sun was burning the last of the early mist off the desert, and the little airfield was slowly emerging from the slumber of darkness. Early starters were busying themselves with their four-seat light planes; walk-rounds to be done and a last-minute check of the flight plan ready for that long-promised trip over the lakes and mountains. The weather as always was almost perfect, with just the hint of a few feathers of cirrostratus.

The *Guardian Angel* was sitting outside the Angel Mustang Company's flight school office; the low morning sun was glinting off her polished aluminium and immaculate scarlet and blue paint scheme. Rusty, oblivious to all around him, was shining the big bubble canopy with a bottle of Perspex polish in one hand and a soft yellow cloth in the other, meticulously removing every suggestion of a smear. Next to the *Guardian Angel* stood her 'sister ship', the *Avenging Angel*. Only a close inspection would reveal any difference between the two. They were both Inglewood-built North American P-51D Mustangs. Both were modified to take two occupants by the removal of a body fuel tank and some antiquated radio gear, plus the addition of a taller fin to help directional stability. The real difference lay in their provenance. The *Avenging Angel* was only a baby; she had first felt the wind beneath her wings in the spring of 1946. Big sister *Guardian Angel* was a real veteran. She had been shipped to England in 1944 and had survived the horrors of the Second World War in the killing skies of German-occupied Northern Europe. Many times she had fired her six 'point five' heavy machine guns and was responsible for the grief of several widows, lovers and mothers. She was a classic killer and, amongst other things, a former member of the elite USAAF 8th Air Force 'Blue Nosed Bastards' from Bodney, Norfolk, England.

The taxi pulled up at the gate and Kirsten paid off the driver and sent him on his way. She stood enjoying the moment. This was going to be a day to remember. Many pilots only dreamed of something like this but few ever got anywhere near it.

Ven was already going over the planned routine for the day and had double-checked both aeroplanes, something he had done a thousand times before. Sufficient fuel – no more, no less – had been loaded; the maintenance log had been checked and signed; the weather was perfect and life was good.

Kirsten walked into the flight line office with the minimum of fuss and sat at the table facing Ven, who was intently studying a large map. Rusty walked in and sat on a battered stool propped at an angle against the wall, holding what was his third coffee of the day. "Too much of that stuff is bad for you, Rusty," but Rusty was not impressed and mumbled something about him sounding like his mother.

Dressed in jeans and a tee-shirt, Kirsten Davies warranted no more than a casual glance. Ven made a quick mental appreciation and then returned to the work in hand: the briefing for the formation aerobatics.

"OK, listen up and listen closely, we are going to start off nice and slow and work up to the more difficult stuff. We have plenty of time and we need to get to know each other." Ven paused, mentally kicking himself for not picking his words more carefully. "Flying-wise, I mean, of course." Kirsten smiled, which annoyed Ven into moving up a gear. "You have to remember the Mustang is no aerobatic special with low weight and plenty of power reserve like a Yak. Treat her with respect and she will take you to heaven. Abuse her and pull her too hard in a turn and she will half snap into a power-on spin which if not recovered could result in her boring a big hole in the ground with you still inside." Rusty looked up from under the peak of his cap, intrigued by the customer-handling skills of his partner.

"We will take off on main runway 120 and make a slow turn towards the south while climbing to 6,000 feet and form up about… here," pointing to a reference point on the map.

"This is well clear of the circuit and I have OK'd it with the tower. To start with, we will just plough up and down this track line, getting a little closer after each heading reversal."

Kirsten nodded. This was a little basic, but she understood his concern.

"Keep your eyes on me at all times, try and fixate on some reference point on my aircraft that you can quickly align with."

"Mr Carlson, I have flown formation aerobatics before, you know." Kirsten regretted that remark immediately but saved the situation with, "Sorry, please carry on," and after a pause, Ven continued.

"Next, we'll try some simple climbing turns and graduate to a wingover or two, and if that works, we can try a well-spaced-out loop, maybe 50 feet apart. At this point, we will stop for some lunch, then, this afternoon, maybe some half and full 'Cubans'. We'll see how it goes and then we can take it from there." Kirsten, who was happy with everything so far, nodded her agreement and Ven continued. "Rusty here will keep an ear open on the VHF and tie things together if there is a problem, which I am sure there won't be."

"Sounds good, I'm ready. Let's go for it then."

Kirsten sat motionless in the *Guardian Angel*; her eyes were scanning to the left and right as well as straight ahead at the instrument panel. The familiarity she had achieved with the machine from the week's work had lowered the tension and excitement of that first day, and she now felt she was firmly in control.

For a moment, she allowed her mind to wander back through the decades and the many pilots who had sat right here where she was, young men hardly in their twenties who flew the *Guardian Angel* for up to eight hours at a time, encumbered by a lumpy parachute and dinghy pack and fighting their individual wars, protecting the Flying Fortresses and Liberators of the 8th Air Force or... strafing airfields at altitudes of 10 feet or less whilst flying through murderous walls of anti-aircraft flack.

She was snapped back into reality by Ven's laconic voice:

"Ready for pre-flight check, Blue Two. We will do this together." She looked across at Ven in the other Mustang. "Affirmative, Blue One."

"OK, master on."

"Check."

"Fuel quantity."

"Check."

"Trim – Set 6 degrees right rudder, aileron and elevator trim 0 degrees."

"Check."

"Controls unlocked and free."

"Check."

"Magnetos."

"Check."

"Radiator coolant door open."

"Check."

"Canopy release – check safety wire."

"Check."

Ven's voice continued with the list until the pre-flight was completed. "OK, looks good, now for the pre-start."

"OK, Blue One. Ready."

Ven ran through the pre-start checklist in the same cool unhurried way as the pre-flight check and then proceeded to the engine start list.

"This is it then. Start checks coming up."

"Fuel pressure 10 lbs/in."

"Check."

"Cold engine prime. Give her six seconds."

"Check."

"Check with the guy out front all clear."

"Check."

"Crank engine – count four blades and Mags to both – mixture to auto lean."

The big propeller groaned as the starter pulled the Rolls-Royce Merlin over, and after a slight hesitation, the engine coughed and burst into life, spewing out orange flames momentarily from the twelve exhaust stacks.

"OK, now adjust the throttle to give a stable 800 RPM."

"Done." Kirsten resisted the urge to add the word already.

"Generator ON."

"Check."

The two Mustangs sat for a moment with the two big props beating in harmony as both pilots monitored temperatures and pressures and carried out power checks and validated the systems.

"We have clearance. Are we ready to move?"

"Ready when you are."

"OK, follow me at a respectful distance and watch out for small stuff that can hide under this long nose." Kirsten grinned and replied in the affirmative as she watched the mechanic remove the chocks from both aeroplanes. Gunning the throttle with his left hand, Ven released the toe brakes and inched out onto the taxiway. The little convoy made its way slowly to the end of runway 120 with the two *Angels* closely spaced behind each other but offset by a safe distance.

"Tower ready to roll."

"OK, blue formation cleared for take-off on runway 120."

Both pilots did another quick check of the essentials, looked at each other and gave the time-honoured thumbs-up.

As Ven worked the RPM up to 2,300 RPM with a boost pressure of 39 ins, the Mustang was straining to be free, and as he released the brakes, she surged forward, looking for her natural environment. "Now keep the tail down until 50 knots, hold that swing." The gyroscopic torque was doing its utmost to pull the aeroplane onto the grass despite the rudder trim and continuous correction. "Bit of forward stick pressure and feed in some more power 55 ins. Wait until 105 knots and rotate her smoothly into the sky."

Ven had done this a hundred times before but he never tired of the thrill. "GEAR UP, power back to 46 ins and 2,700 RPM climb away at 150 knots and relax."

Slightly behind him, Kirsten had mirrored his every movement as the gap slowly narrowed. Together, the two *Angels* climbed steadily away and turned slowly towards the blue-edged mountains in the distance.

The two Mustangs moved as one. From a distance, they appeared to form the two extremities of a single entity. The years of practice and experience were showing through, and compared to his mood earlier that morning, Ven was quite relaxed. Conditions were perfect and the two machines were behaving faultlessly, enabling an easy trust to form between the two pilots.

"OK, we will try one more loop before calling a break for lunch." His breezy mood was now very relaxed and they were both enjoying themselves. "Close up to 15 feet and we will really nail it this time." The two aircraft gently dipped their noses and started to build up speed in a shallow dive, then arched up into a ballistic vertical in exactly the same way they had done many times that morning. As gravity started to suck away the speed, the two Mustangs pulled through the vertical to the 'inverted', neatly locked together in perfect synchronisation; poetry in motion, pilot and machine in harmony.

In the canopy retaining rails support structure of the *Guardian Angel*, a small scratch had been working on a stress fracture for sixty years and finally... at last... it got its own way. The rail let go with an almighty crack which in turn allowed a powerful rush of air under the Perspex bubble. No contest... In a split second, the canopy ripped itself free, cleaving a murderous gash through Kirsten's helmet, rendering her unconscious.

In the *Avenging Angel*, Ven received no warning at all, but out of the corner of his eye, he registered the flash of the flying canopy and then froze and watched, mesmerised, as his flying partner leaned away from him and entered a steep spiralling spin, which if unchecked could only have one outcome.

In the airfield club bar, Rusty was sinking his third whisky chaser and thinking how good life was; a few hours by himself and a freedom away from Ven's continual gaze and prodding. The portable VHF on the bar suddenly crackled into life. It was the tower. "Rusty, one of your two aeroplanes has an emergency, seems to be some sort of control problem. We have got a full emergency going. Horseback has radioed in that BLUE 2 is spinning in just south of Red Ridge. I'll patch you in."

Back in the air, Ven was trying everything he knew to stay with the falling BLUE 2.

"Kirsten… spin recovery now. For Christ's sake, put the stick in the corner now!"

The altimeter was unwinding rapidly, 5,000 feet to go. He felt so helpless; there must be something he could do but his brain was not answering the call and he just kept repeating his plea. There were only seconds to go now and he was already lower than he should be, but he was determined to ride this thing all the way down, reefing the Mustang into tighter and tighter turns.

Eventually, auto self-preservation took over and at the last second he flattened out and pulled away to the north with one last fleeting glance at Kirsten's lifeless body, head pressed hard against the instrument panel, still alive but for how long?

Ven's mind had memorised the predicted point of impact and with a heavy heart he turned through 180 degrees and made his way back, scanning the ground for the inevitable plume of smoke with a murderous orange glow at its base, but nothing… nothing at all. Things were not making sense in this nightmare. Circling, he kept on looking and then he saw it… a small black dot racing back towards the airfield. Could it be that the unbelievable had happened, some sort of miraculous recovery? It had to be the *Guardian Angel*. He shoved the throttle forward and raced after the speck in the distance. It had a good lead and he doubted he would catch it before the airfield.

Every steel muscle in the old Chevy pick-up was straining as hard as it could to get Rusty back to the airfield office where by rights he should already have been. As he rounded the threshold fence, he glanced quickly away to the left and, sure enough, there was the unmistakeable form of a P-51 on approach, which didn't make sense. Surely, Ven would have stayed close to the incident so that he could direct the rescue services! He stopped the truck and stared at the approaching shape; flaps down, gear down. It looked OK but there was something odd, not quite right. Was it the slightly-lower-than-normal nose down attitude or was it that, to his eye, the smooth-flowing contour of the Mustang's back was broken? Things were not making much sense and the whisky was not helping. "Hell, it's not right. The canopy is not just slid back, it's completely missing. This has got to be the damaged aircraft, but… where is Ven?"

He looked again to the east and, sure enough, there was a second aircraft, little more than a speck but streaking back low and fast at no more than 500 feet. As Rusty turned his attention again to the damaged Mustang, his heart missed a beat. He could hardly see the pilot's head, so how in hell was she still in control? But she must be, because the approach was perfect. There was something else strange about the look of the crippled aircraft, but what was it? Rusty blinked hard and opened his eyes, but the moment had passed, and the cockpit was obscured as the aircraft moved away from him. Transfixed, he continued to stare as the Mustang gently settled onto the tarmac. Confusion took hold for a moment but not for long as he gunned the Chevy along the perimeter road. He just had to be there when it came to a stop.

The *Guardian Angel* came to a halt with little fuss at the far end of the runway. In fact, it had been almost a textbook landing.

Rusty and the fire wagon arrived almost simultaneously at the stationary *Guardian Angel,* where he and a fireman bounded up onto the wing. Rusty froze, his senses completely shot. The fireman was trying to get the pilot out and shouting to Rusty for help, but all he could do was mumble, "How did this happen, how did this happen?" as Kirsten lay slumped in the front seat, head forward, covered in blood, gently moaning.

Turning about, he searched the field for any clues, but all he could see was sand and weeds. At this point, Rusty's world started to spin, and he fell backwards over the flaps in a crumpled heap onto the hard tarmac.

Seconds later, as a confused Rusty was still fighting to comprehend the situation, a joyous Ven flashed overhead in the *Avenging Angel.*

*

Ven and Rusty sat together in the hospital waiting room, trying to digest the mixture of anxiety and relief. This was one large puzzle, and none of it made any sense.

"Rusty, have you completely lost it? What the hell have you been drinking? Nobody is going to believe what you're saying or what you think you saw. It's best we keep it simple and stick with what we know happened."

"Honest, Ven, I know what you're thinking. You think it was the drink but on my grandmother's life, I only had a couple... I'm simply telling you what I thought I saw."

"You useless bastard, I've lost count how many grandmothers you've had. What was it this time? Beer and whisky chasers?"

"Just a couple," he lied again.

"And you were the only person to observe this miracle?"

"Go ask the bartender, he will vouch for me. I was definitely OK when I left the club."

"You two are as thick as thieves. Whenever I ask, it's always, *just a couple.*" Curbing his anger, Rusty looked straight ahead and murmured, "Right now, I think we should just be grateful that the customer is alive and not sat here arguing about what did or did not happen. There will be plenty of time for that later, and just remember you were up there, not me."

The two of them settled into an uneasy silence which was only broken by the opening of the polished wooden door at the far end of the room, through which a doctor appeared wearing a well-practised expression that gave little away.

"Give us the news, Doc, the way it is. At the moment, we are the nearest thing she has to friend or family and we feel kind of responsible." After a short pause, Rusty added, "In fact, we're... totally responsible."

"Well, it could be much worse. She has a severe contusion stretching halfway over her head and she will have a grade 'A' headache when she wakes up, which isn't going to go away in a hurry. We have completed the skin repairs, and nature and a long period of rest should heal the outside, and with a little luck, her hair will cover the scarring. As for the inside and the psychological effects, well, no two of these head injuries are the same. The long-term mental effects of a trauma like this are completely unpredictable, only time will tell. By the way, the metal helmet she was wearing saved her life. Let that be a lesson to you macho 'leather helmet' for authenticity types!"

Ven looked down at his feet, completely lost as to what to say next, then after a short pause: "Is she conscious?"

"No... she was, but at the moment she is under heavy sedation... I would suggest you come back in twenty-four hours. By then, we will be able to tell you a whole lot more. If there are any further developments, I will let you know."

Ven dropped Rusty off and returned to his rundown bachelor's house on the outskirts of town. He parked the truck and sat on the living-room couch for three hours, turning things over and over in his mind, trying to make some sense of what had happened. Mercifully, the fading adrenaline eventually subsided, dropping him into a fitful sleep.

*

Days came and went and Kirsten made good progress. The only visible outward sign she wore was the scar on her scalp, slowly being covered by soft new hair. Her father had visited her in hospital and flown back to England. Her company had told her to take as much time off as she needed, and mercifully the insurance company were paying the medical fees.

Ven had told the investigators, friends and colleagues alike, that she must have 'come to' just in time to pull the Mustang out of the spin and had managed to recover to Desert Field before passing out again shortly after bringing it to a halt. He certainly was not happy with this explanation, but it was the only one that fitted. He made no mention of Rusty's story, and Rusty himself never mentioned it again. Life returned to normal and so did the business, which did not seem to suffer as a result of the incident, which they tried to play down. In fact, after all the mandatory checks, the damaged Mustang was flying again within weeks, with new rails and the spare canopy.

After leaving hospital, Kirsten spent some time on the Californian coast with Ven, a constant but slightly remote companion, leaving (the now teetotal) Rusty to run the business. Ven stayed at an apartment nearby and was always available when needed. Kirsten talked quite openly about the past and future, but in all the time they were in each other's company, she never mentioned the accident once, which suited Ven, who although desperately needing closure had never come to terms with what had happened that day.

Eight days into her two weeks' Californian recuperation, she surprised him with a request. "Don't you think it's about time you took me out to dinner, or do I still look too much like something out of an old Frankenstein horror movie?" Ven smiled and replied that of course he would. The thought occurred to him that maybe, just maybe, this nightmare was coming to an end!

"OK, see you tomorrow night. I will pick you up at about eight. Oh, by the way, I don't have my dinner jacket with me."

Kirsten grinned. "No problem. I don't have my evening gown either!"

*

The following night, Ven took her to 'Tweeters on the Beach', a place that had been recommended to him by an old buddy. A soft sea breeze was blowing and the sky was big, black and filled with stars.

Halfway into the lobster, she asked him the question he had been dreading. "What really happened that day, Ven? My memory is just a blank from the moment the canopy hit me to waking up in hospital. The doctors thought it was absolutely incredible that I could have made such a recovery, partial or otherwise, so soon after being struck. I remember looping up into that beautiful late-morning sun and then… Nothing."

Ven drew air in through his slightly clenched teeth before replying after a considerable pause.

"What would you say if I told you that your canopy detached, knocked you completely senseless, that you then entered a spin that should have proved fatal, but somehow, and I don't know how, something got you out of that spin and placed you back on the ground at Desert Field?"

Kirsten looked at Ven incredulously. "What do you mean, something?"

Ven turned away and then turned back. "All I know is that I was way below safe altitude when I pulled out, and as I recollect, at that moment in time, you had a face full of instrument panel. Please don't ask me again, because I have no answers. There is very little in life which freaks me out, but the mere mention of this is giving me cold shivers just thinking about it." He held his head in his hands and stared down at the table, unsure as to what to say next. Kirsten leaned across the table and held his wrist… Ven looked up. "What is important is that you made a fantastic recovery, and right now I am so enjoying being here with you… God, that sounded corny."

Kirsten smiled warmly and added, "Don't beat yourself up so much. Sometimes, a girl likes corny." They both laughed, paused, sipped their wine and finished the lobster.

*

The following morning, Ven was woken by his phone. It was years since he had overslept. What was happening to his well-ordered life? It was Kirsten: "Hi, Ven, great news. They have given me the all-clear to fly home next week."

Ven replied with the words he was supposed to say but secretly inside he was hurting a little. He had become quite fond of Kirsten but that was life; certain things were beyond your control. He knew he had to be back at Desert Field on Monday for the FAA Annual Inspection and there was plenty of work to do before then, but he could be back here on the Californian coast by Tuesday. "What day is your flight?"

"Midday, Wednesday. Why do you ask?"

"I just thought we could have dinner together on the Tuesday evening, maybe the last chance we'll get for some time."

Kirsten considered and then replied, "Is it today or tomorrow you are off back to Desert Field?"

"Well, I was thinking about getting a head start and setting off today. I hate to think what carnage Rusty has caused." This was unkind; Rusty had proved perfectly capable of running the business in his absence.

"Well, it would be nice to meet up one more time before I leave."

"OK, it's a date then." Ven put the phone down and reflected. This was against all his normal self-imposed rules. Was he getting too involved?

*

The annual inspection went well. Ven had expected loads of questions from the authorities about the incident and he was not disappointed. There was nothing more he could tell them about how the *Guardian Angel* had recovered to Desert Field, so, in the end, they had no choice but to reluctantly accept his account. On the technical side, he was on far more familiar ground and his explanation of the canopy rail failure and the subsequent Non-Destructive Testing (NDT) was accepted without question. Rusty, true to his word, had stayed off the drink and Ven now felt more confident leaving him to run the company, which as an equal partner, of course, he was perfectly entitled to do.

"Well, this is it then, the end of my big adventure." Kirsten was sat opposite him looking very attractive in a cream-coloured sleeveless top and black trousers. Ven had brought his Tux this time, but when he'd tried it on, a quick glance in the mirror had convinced him he looked more like a bear in a straitjacket, so had decided to keep it simple and was sporting an open-necked cotton shirt and a new pair of dark slacks.

"It was certainly different, that's for sure. Only wish it had not involved all the trauma. I know I have no need to say it but... I still feel guilty about the whole thing."

"Ven, there is no need... Actually, I feel incredibly lucky."

"Is flying still for you? Nobody would blame you if you just walked away."

"Try and stop me, and anyway, I don't know anything else. Sure, there will be plenty of tests to pass and hurdles to jump before they clear me to fly commercially again, but I don't have nightmares about what happened, if that's what you mean. I guess that's one advantage of having no recollection at all of the last part of that flight." The waiter appeared and they ordered their meal, she having the langoustine and pasta and he a steak. Whilst they were waiting, Kirsten tried to learn a little more about Ven by asking questions she hadn't tried before. "Ven seems to be an unusual name, is it short for something?"

"Well, actually, it's short for Venezuela, quite simple really. You see, my mother was from South America and my father's family was from Norway, so that's me... Ven Carlson."

"You have never talked of your parents before and I notice you used the past tense just then. I'm guessing there is some sadness."

"Well, I loved them both, but Dad smoked himself to death and my mother died of a broken heart. She couldn't live without him."

"Sorry, Ven, I should not have pushed you."

"No problem, I had them both for twenty-five years. Dad was a pilot in the military, so we moved around a lot."

"Did you ever get to Europe?"

"Sure, we were in Germany for two years, but one of my regrets was that I never got to England."

"Maybe we could fix that one day."

Ven laughed. "Believe it or not, I have had a chance or two."

"How do you mean?"

"The big Summer Air Show they hold near Cambridge every year, they like to invite guest display pilots, and with ten or fifteen Mustangs on show, pilots with a display authorisation are in big demand, but it's a hell of a long way to go, and it's peak season for us."

"But I came all the way here."

"That's true. I'll definitely give it some thought if the chance comes up again."

"And how about your two Mustangs? How did you come by them?"

"My father rebuilt the *Guardian Angel* from a wreck. He had recently retired from the Air Force and found her down in El Salvador, bought her for next to nothing. All my spare time as a boy was spent helping him rebuild her. You wouldn't believe the hours we put in. We had lots of help, of course, and eventually we finished her. One of the spin-offs was that by the time we got her ready for her first flight, we had the makings of a small company with a full-time Airframe and Power Plant mechanic, we could call on. But rebuilding vintage aeroplanes isn't cheap, and the family were existing on his Air Force pension and his savings. We had virtually no other income, but my father was a stubborn son of a... I apologise, got a little lost with my words there, and he saw it through, but his forty-a-day habit and the stress of it all meant his days were numbered."

Ven looked away to compose himself and Kirsten interjected. "Sorry, Ven, I can see this is hard for you. There is no need to go on."

"Just look at me, the big tough Ven Carlson, afraid of nothing and about to weep like a babe." He paused and then carried on. "Anyway, early on, we had decided to use the Mustang as a business venture, so we had the big bubble canopy and the second seat fitted as well as the vertical stabiliser extension. Looking back now, I can see what he was doing. A P-51D Mustang with her pedigree will now sell for well over a million bucks. He knew his years were numbered and he was trying to provide Ma and me with financial security.

"Anyway, the business took off in a way you could never have imagined. Living near the airfield had one big positive though – he taught me to fly in a Cessna 150 he used to borrow from an old Air Force buddy he knew on the field. Would you believe, I held a pilot's licence before a driver's licence. On the downside, although I completed high school, I missed out on a college education. Flying was all I wanted to do, and practice made perfect. When the cancer finally got him, I was already checked out on the *Angel* and could hold my own with most of the weekend warriors."

Kirsten nodded. "Where does Rusty fit into all this?"

"He was one of our first customers and got fully bitten by the bug." Ven chuckled to himself. "Looking at him now, you wouldn't believe it, but his family are not just loaded, they are sinking in oil money, so to keep him happy his father bought him the other Mustang on condition that a reputable maintenance outfit looked after it, and that was us."

Kirsten took another sip of her wine and carried on. "So getting together and forming a joint company with two aeroplanes was the obvious way to go."

"Absolutely. Rusty has a few failings, which you may have noticed, but actually he is a very good pilot, although

I doubt if he will ever reach the very top. His real talent lies in handling customers. He's a real people person, something I am definitely not... Anyway, Miss Davies, the last five minutes have been all about me... how about you?"

Kirsten was far shorter with her answer than she intended. "What do you want to know?"

"Ouch, that's a bit below the belt, but you know what, without asking, I've told you most of my life story, so I will leave the answer of that question to you." Kirsten was aware she had been unfair in pushing Ven so hard, but what could she do now? The damage was done.

"No, I'm at fault. If I had half an ounce of common sense, I should have steered the conversation away from something that was obviously hurting."

The waiter was back with their main courses. Kirsten was trying to repair the damage. "If this tastes as good as it looks, well!"

After their plates were removed and they were waiting for coffee, Kirsten decided to open up. "Going on how little time he spent with me when I was in hospital, you've probably worked out that my father and I are not that close."

"There must be a good reason."

"Well, that's the strange thing. It's probably more to do with the woman he is married to."

"Your mother!"

"No, my mother is dead. She died when I was five, killed in an RTA."

"RTA?"

"Road Traffic Accident. Sorry, I get that from my father. He's a senior police officer."

"I see, stepmother and authoritarian father. Not a good combo, I guess."

Kirsten went on to explain that she had been told that her real mother, although a very capable and successful businesswoman, had one failing and that was fast cars. She died, ironically, not due to any driving mistake she made but at the wheel of her beloved Jaguar XK150 on a dual carriageway, when a driver going the other way lost control on an icy bend and careered through the centre reservation, slamming into her.

"Wow. So both of us have lost parents but you were only five. Do you have any memories of her?"

"Only a few. She was beautiful and I know that's true because I still have pictures of her."

"Ah, here is the coffee... I tell you what, Kirsten." He contemplated for several seconds.

"Go on."

"Well, whichever way you look at it, tonight hasn't been a big success, has it? All we have managed to do is conjure up some very hurtful memories which we then preceded to inflict on each other."

"But, Ven, at least we've been honest."

"True, but tell you what, let's have something a little stronger and then I'll walk you back to your hotel."

The short walk back to the hotel where she was staying was over in minutes. Although they walked close, side by side, it was conducted almost in silence.

They stood in the packed hotel foyer, where a bus from a late flight arrival had just divested itself of fifty noisy passengers. Kirsten led Ven over to the lift but stopped just short of it. "I guess this is goodbye then."

Ven didn't know what to say. Was this the end? Would he never see her again? "Guess so, but promise me you will keep in touch and give me a call when you get back home."

The lift bell rang and the doors opened. He put his arm around her and they kissed each other on the cheek. The doors closed and she was gone. He brushed his cheek as he breathed in; he could still smell her scent.

TWO

Rose Collins looked about her to make sure she was truly alone and then sprang into the air, performing a very unladylike skip, but then that was Rose all over; she had never wanted to be a lady. She had given her mother and father a torrid time ever since she was little. First, there were the bad reports from school, then the bird nesting and apple *scrumping* incidents, not to mention the public scrap which resulted in a local boy two years her senior sporting a black eye for a week. Jane Collins was well aware that Rose was different but adored her daughter all the more for it and chose to ignore the local postmistress, Miss Watts, when many years ago, she had commented, "I do worry about Rose, Mrs Collins. She does not seem to fit in like the other village girls. Why, she only attended the cooking and needlework club once and we never saw her again. It's such a shame considering the way your two boys have turned out, a real credit to the village, they are."

29

Jane, who in a way also secretly and jealously admired her daughter's outlook on life, had bitten her lip and stifled a quick reply, preferring, "Don't you worry about Rose, Miss Watts. She will be fine, you just wait and see!"

Now six years later and in the last of her teenage years, Rose was still an enigma. Her body had developed into that of a very attractive young woman but the rebellious streak was still there, and in her own mind, she was absolutely determined that she, Rose, would not follow the well-trodden track of other village girls. A trip up the aisle to the church altar and the drudgery of bringing up a young family in wartime were not for her. The boys liked her and she liked the boys, but she kept them at a good arm's length.

On top of Water Tower Hill, the big East Anglian sky did not disappoint. People said you could see several counties from this modest hill, not just Suffolk, but Cambridge, Norfolk and maybe Essex as well. The azure blue sky was as clear as a bell, although over to the distant east some great castles of summer cumulonimbus were starting to build. Rose closed her eyes and breathed in the pure country air, letting the soft summer breeze wash over her. This had always been her favourite place, well away from the village and separated from it by the ancient woodlands she had wandered as a child. The only building in sight was the redbrick Victorian water tower, a landmark that could be seen from miles around. On this grassy knoll, she had been queen of the castle, a place where she could let her imagination wander and run riot without limits.

As she sat there staring into the distance, she was aware of a small movement on the horizon. Rose mused, what could that be? Surely not an aeroplane, although God knows there were enough of them in the three counties. People said you could not go more than a handful of miles in any direction in East Anglia without coming across a military airfield. But yes, it was an aeroplane flying very low and very fast. Rose's mind went into panic mode. Could it be a lone German raider like the one that had flattened the local nearby town's high street? "It can't be, surely not. There hasn't been a raid now for over a year." Transfixed, she just watched the shape getting bigger and bigger. "Good grief. It's coming straight at me – why me? This is so unfair." Automatically, she threw herself to the ground as it wheeled around the tower. Opening her eyes, she relaxed. "Of course it's not after me. It's just using the water tower as a turning point."

The P-51D Mustang, glinting bright blue and silver in the sun, was coming back now but much more slowly. The cockpit canopy was slid back and the pilot was giving her a cheery wave of apology. Without thinking, she waved back. It circled once more and then departed in the same direction it had come from, slowly disappearing over the ocean fields of waving golden late-summer wheat. Rose was still tingling with excitement as she turned and strolled back down the hill, her imagination running riot. What must it be like, to be master of the air and fly like that!

She was in no hurry as she kept to the dusty footpath that led to a lane which in turn meandered its way to the village high street. Walking along the street, which at this point had more horse chestnut trees on each side than cottages, she became aware of movement in the canopy of one of the trees. Having a good idea of what it was, being early August, she did not look up but stopped when she was underneath it. "John Arbon, come on down before you fall out of that tree and kill yourself. The conkers won't be ready yet, you must wait until they fall naturally."

"Sorry, Miss Rose, I wanted to be the first at school on Monday with a brand-new one on a string."

"That's as may be, but the secret to that, young John, is to get up early and see what has freshly fallen. Now get on home, before I tell your mother." The miscreant knew when he was beat and meekly obeyed before disappearing down the street, leaving Rose smiling and thinking, *Not long ago that would have been me.*

She reached home, which was a small but comfortable cottage. As she opened the gate, she was confronted by her father. "And where have you been, young lady? I could have done with a hand here," pointing at the vegetable patch. "If your brothers had been here, I wouldn't have needed to ask. Both of them would have rolled up their sleeves and got on with it." Rose was in no mood for an argument.

"Dad, I work in an office all week and at the weekend I like to get a bit of fresh air. What's wrong with that..." She paused before continuing and immediately regretting, "It's not my fault for not being born a boy. You and Mum have got something to do with that."

Her father smashed his gardening fork hard into the ground and started marching towards her, before being arrested by a firm voice from the open kitchen window. "Jack, you leave that girl be. She works just as hard as anyone of her age in this village." An uneasy truce settled between the two, which resulted in both parties apologising to each other.

Rose walked into the kitchen, where her mother placed her arms around her. "Don't fret, Rose. He doesn't mean it, just a little bit tired, that's all."

"He'll never understand. I don't want to be just Rose Collins. I want to be someone. I want to do something with my life."

"Anyway, apart from that, did you see anybody when you were out walking?"

Rose sat at the kitchen table and retold the exciting happenings on Water Tower Hill.

"That's lovely, Rose. Now give me a hand at shelling these peas."

*

Captain Domenico D'Angelino was feeling tired but happy as he put the Mustang into a smooth curved approach, which lined the sleek fighter up with USAAF fighter station 391 Linton Grange. This was his home base and he had volunteered, even though he was on 'stand down', to collect and air-test this much-needed and freshly repaired replacement aircraft from the nearby station 141 at Bodney.

As he jumped off the wing of the Mustang, he could not help but overhear his crew chief, Dick Ferra, mumbling to his assistant: "Why do we always get the 'second-hand Rose'? I'd put my last dollar on betting that those headline boys over at Bodney have nothing but rows of shiny new ships."

Dom turned and reassured his mechanics. "Don't worry, boys. I've just put her through her paces and she won't be found wanting. Give me an aeroplane with a few proven hours on the clock any time. Look at that big skin repair on the port main-plane, she's a survivor, all right. You mark my words."

The crew chief nodded and then asked a question. "I can see that, Dom, sir, and to be honest I don't think she is that old, plus she has already had the fin filet modification done, which is more than most of our early D models have. Kind of strange they should let us have her, though!"

Dom replied, "You're right, you know, but as always there is a story. Apparently, the new group executive over there brought her with him when he was transferred to Bodney. He did a couple of missions with her but then he and his wingman were jumped by a pack of Fw190s when low on fuel. They both got beat up a bit. However, as luck would have it, the 'Blue Nosers' were due some brand-new replacements so, as you would expect, the 'exec' was assigned one of those, meaning after repair the *Angel* here was surplus to requirements, so when our engineering officer heard about it, we grabbed her."

"Sounds good. Will this ship be assigned to you, Dom, sir?"

"I think so, I must be one of the last pilots in the squadron with an old C model and the boss has agreed. She handles like a peach and that Packard Merlin is a real honey. Tell you what, get the painter to get that blue-nosed stuff off of the nose and replace it with our purple checks, but leave her name as it is... No, on second thoughts, do you think he could squeeze in the word *Guardian* before *Angel*? I rather like that. *Guardian Angel*. Let's hope she'll look after me."

Ferra nodded and grinned. "Sure thing, Dom, sir. I'll see what I can do."

Captain Domenico D'Angelino was known to everyone as Dom or Don, but that didn't worry him at all; he answered to both. Yes, he was of Italian descent but, unlike his family, he saw himself as an American not an American Italian. Family was important but not everything. His father and his family had suffered hard times in the Depression and had given up a lot to see Domenico through college. His father was not pleased when he had gone against his wishes and joined the Army as an aviation cadet and not the Navy, which would have been his preference but... in his heart of hearts, he knew that whatever Domenico did, he was a D'Angelino, and he would do it well.

Yes, the family had seen hard times but they had come through it. Dom had done well, very well; not only was he an excellent flyer but he was blessed with those rare qualities of natural-born leadership and the controlled aggression so necessary in a fighter pilot. Dom D'Angelino inside and outside the cockpit were two very different animals. Some said that once seated in a P-51, he grew a pair of devil horns, but back on the ground you could not wish to meet a more mild-mannered individual. Promotion had been rapid and at the tender age of twenty-three, he was not only a captain but also a flight leader. On a couple of occasions when the group CO, exec officer or squadron commanders were not scheduled to fly, he had led the forty-eight fighters which made up the fighter group on its mission, escorting the big bombers deep into Germany. Dom had been in the Air Force for over two years but only in England for seven months, and he had learned quickly, very quickly, and yes, he had already lost some good friends along the way.

One of them, Brizio, had joined up with him. They had gone through basic and advanced training together and when the two of them had been sent to the ETO (European Theatre of Operations), they had found themselves posted to the same squadron in England as two greenhorn replacement pilots. Brizio was a natural, confident and gifted pilot, but his one failing would lead to his undoing. He was a born showman, not only with the local girls but also in the air. His victory tally was exceptional and he only needed one more to make ACE status, the first pilot in the squadron to achieve five victories. He got that fifth victory in a hard-fought turning fight with an Me109 over Northern France, but his celebratory beat-up of his home base on return ended in tragedy when his propeller clipped the roof of the chequered runway control vehicle, causing the crippled fighter to plough into two visiting parked P-47s.

The death of his best friend had a sobering effect on Domenico D'Angelino. He rejected the frantic social life of his fellow squadron pilots, not for him the riotous trips to London and Piccadilly, or the fitting of a red silk lining to his best uniform. That was their safety valve and for them it worked, but Dom, who had tried London a couple of times, was not convinced, and he always felt a slight outsider. Maybe he was just a little too homespun. Sure, he had friends enough and was well respected, but what little leisure time he had was spent reading or walking in the local countryside. On the surface, he was calm, but the strain and pressures were tremendous and long ago he had decided that to survive he needed to be one hundred per cent fit, both in his body and his head.

Three months into his time in England he had received the dreaded *Dear John* letter from his girl back home, a girl he had been dating since leaving high school. He had blamed himself for that. How dumb could he really be, telling her in that last letter home *not to waste her life and wait for him*! He had dated a WAC Air Controller and she was great fun, but there were several other airmen who appeared also to be having great fun with her, so… right now, he was unattached, which seemed to suit for the time being.

THREE

THE MISSION

The voice of the junior intelligence officer shattered his dream state. "Rise and shine, sir. Mission is on, breakfast in thirty minutes."

Dom rubbed the sleep from his eyes and stared at the floor. "Hell, why on earth do they have to fight this war in the middle of the night!" He had shaved the night before because he had known what was coming; that at least was one less task he had to do. He stretched and dragged himself to the washroom, which was full of fellow half-asleep bodies, got dressed into his usual multiple layers, slipped into his leather jacket and set off for breakfast on his jealously guarded and hard-won bicycle.

There was a familiarity with the routine that followed, but as today he was not to be the mission or squadron leader, there was no need to attend group operations to plan tactics and study mission data. He did, however, check in at the ops room desk to see what position he was flying, knowing full well anything else he needed to know would be fully divulged at the general briefing.

He propped his bicycle against the green corrugated officers' mess hall wall and made his way to the same table he always used. Breakfast never changed; powdered eggs, toast, fruit juice and coffee, and, as always, he ate it but with no enjoyment. He had been through this routine many times before, but it always dulled his appetite. Looking about him, he could see that different pilots behaved in different ways; some wolfed down everything they could, others were maybe… more like him.

He registered a voice from across the table. "Morning, Captain." It was 2nd Lt Pepperman, one of the replacement pilots, obviously very nervous and pushing the bright yellow globs of powdered egg around his plate.

"What's this, Pepperman? You have been bugging the CO to be put on a bomber escort mission for weeks."

Pepperman looked up and forced a smile. "I guess it's only just hit home that this is it. Everyone tells me that I will learn more today than all those months in flight school and… well… I don't want to screw up and let anybody down."

Dom tried to reassure him. "Don't worry about being afraid. Actually, it's being scared that keeps us all alive, and we have all been there in your position," followed by and immediately regretting, "well, except for the unlucky ones."

Pepperman didn't seem to notice. "I just don't want to be the front-page spread in my home-town weekly newspaper: *Local Airman Dies on His First Mission*."

Dom needed to get this boy back on an even keel because if he carried on like this, one of the medical officers would take notice. "I've seen you fly, you're good, way above average. Sure as hell, they'll pair you up with one of the experienced flight leaders as a wingman. Just remember that when he says this is what we're going to do, that's what you're going to do, OK."

Pepperman relaxed and took a big bite out of his toast. "Thanks, Captain. What was it they used to say? *'Listen and learn. If you don't, you won't.'*"

Dom continued. "Once you close the canopy, you will be right in the zone. Nothing else will matter, believe me... so... see you later."

The pilots who would be flying today clambered aboard the waiting Jeeps to be taken away to the general briefing. For no real reason, the little Jeeps were way overloaded, with men hanging off the back and sides and some even sitting on the engine hood. There was nothing new in this. It was a routine they followed every time, with the same one-liner jokes and same forced laughter and song.

Dom walked into the briefing room. He was early so he sat down and picked up a copy of the *Stars and Stripes*, but he had seen that edition before. Glancing over to the left at the squadron roster board, he searched for his name just to confirm what he already knew and sure enough there it was: 'Red Flight Leader' of four P-51s. What he saw next was a bit of a surprise. His usual wingman, Lt Victor Gilburtson, had been promoted to element leader and would now fly Number 3 in the four-ship flight formation, with Dave Zetterval flying as Gilburtson's wingman at Number 4, but guess who was going to fly at Number 2. Dom's wingman, yes sir, he could have seen this coming, it was none other than 2nd Lt Pepperman. Still, not a problem. At least this way he could keep an eye on him.

Pepperman came in, looking confident but pensive, so Dom waved him over to take the seat next to him. "Wow, it must be my lucky day getting to fly next to one of the best on my first escort mission."

Dom turned towards him. "Now let's get something straight here, Pepperman. This is going to be no cakewalk, it never is. Once we're airborne, I don't want to see any heroics from you. Your job is to guard my tail at all times. Sure, we all look after each other, but you have to remember that as a group, our one aim is to protect the bombers. Is that one hundred per cent clear?" Pepperman nodded.

Dom continued. "Understand, success today is going to be both of us getting back here preferably in one piece and not full of holes, got it?"

Pepperman nodded his understanding once more and pulled out a pen and small notebook to make a note of any important timings that might come up in the briefing. Dom turned to him and said, "Don't do that, can't you see the others are laughing at you?"

"I kind of thought it was a good idea."

"It is but what happens if you drop your precious book in the middle of a fight, then where will you be? Just write the important times like engine start, take-off time, rendezvous time, etc., on the back of your left hand. That way, you will never lose them."

Pepperman was yet again in the act of nodding when the room was hushed by the intelligence officer, who pulled back the mission curtain to reveal a giant map with several narrow ribbons stretched across it. This drew a gasp from the seated pilots; the bombing mission today was to the freight car assembly plant at Magdeburg, not that far from Berlin. It would be the job of this fighter group to take over from the shorter-range P-47 Thunderbolts at a predetermined map reference point and escort the B-17s Fortresses to the target. This had the makings of a very, very long mission trip.

The briefing followed the usual sequence, with the duty intelligence officer reviewing the entire mission, detailing the times and rendezvous points whilst also indicating on the wall map where heavy flak or concentrations of enemy fighters could be expected. He was followed by the staff weather officer, who was listened to with great interest, as on occasion the weather could be a greater threat than German fighters. The usual standard joke was cracked by some wag that, "The weather office is one hundred per cent correct fifty per cent of the time," which got the usual laughter. Finally, the group CO, Colonel Danders, who would be the group leader of the three squadrons today, took to the stage and recapped the important points, stressing that although today any hostiles could be followed through the bomber formations even if they tried one of their new tactics of attacking almost vertically from the front and above the bomber formations, ground strafing on the way home was not an option, as fuel reserves would be low. As the group leader, what he said was law and nobody from the floor challenged him. After taking any last-minute questions, he called for the synchronisation of watches and wished them all luck for today's mission.

Dom turned to Pepperman with a smile on his face. "OK, kid, this is what Uncle Sam pays us for... so let's go."

They piled onto the Jeeps and set off for the squadron ready room where they turned in any personal possessions like letters or photographs to the S2 officer and collected their flight clothing. The locker-room orderly handed them their helmets, flying goggles, oxygen masks, flight overalls, Mae West life jackets, gloves (multiple pairs of gloves, including gauntlets), GI lace-up boots, if required, and their B8 backpack parachutes. Some of the older hands had acquired sheepskin-lined RAF flying boots, helmets and goggles. Some even tucked a .45 handgun or a knife into their boots. More popular, though, was candy and cigarettes for the return trip home. In the squadron ready room, the four flight leaders handed out the course check sheets, maps and escape kits, which they dutifully placed in the various pockets of their flight overalls.

Dom was well aware that the squadron medical officer was not only keeping a keen eye on any of the replacement pilots but was also watching everyone for excessive nervous behaviour or other tell-tale signs of combat fatigue. He tried to relax Pepperman with some throwaway conversation and a final run-through of the course cards. With twenty minutes to go before engine start, the squadron c/o waited for the S2 to confirm that everyone was wearing their identification dog tags and then called, "OK, time to move," and the pilots carried their equipment to the vehicles waiting outside.

On the line, the *Guardian Angel* was being prepared for the mission, resplendent in her new paint job. Crew Chief Dick Ferra, who had been up half the night making sure everything was perfect, was justifiably proud of what he and his fellow mechanics had achieved. A copy of the rectified defects 'form 1' was sitting on the seat for Dom's attention, and his assistant was finally winning the battle of polishing the cockpit Perspex bubble against the moisture of a dewy English summer early morning.

With fifteen minutes to go before engine start, the combined sound of raucous singing and vehicle engine noise signalled the arrival of the pilots at the dispersal. Dom placed his parachute and helmet on the tailplane of his P-51 and then accompanied by Sgt Ferra started a 'visual walk-round' of the aeroplane, knowing full well that everything would be perfect. There was a lot of light-hearted banter, with Dick Ferra reminding him he still owed him five bucks from months ago so he had better come back.

Next door, 2nd Lt Pepperman was going through a similar sequence, although his crew chief was old and wise enough not to make him any more nervous than he already was by commenting on whether this was his first mission or not. Looking along the line, Pepperman noticed that many pilots were having a last-minute pee and decided to follow suit. Just before he climbed onto the wing root, his crew chief gave him one last bit of advice. "See the tailwheel there, sir, always best to note its position before you start. If it's not straight, you could get an embarrassing swing on taxi out."

"Fine, thank you, Sergeant. Anything else I should know?"

"Not really, sir, good luck and have a safe trip."

The pilots started to clamber aboard their respective fighters wearing their backpack chutes. Some had already attached the dinghy, which would form their seat cushion, whilst others had placed the dinghy in the seat and then attached it once they had got in the cockpit. All of them checked that the chute D-ring and operating mechanism were OK, as any damage or distorted hardware could prevent the safe opening of a chute.

Their quick-release safety straps were fastened and checked by their crew chiefs. Next, they donned their helmets and masks, making sure the electrical jacks for the radio and earphones were plugged into their respective plug sockets. Finally, the mask oxygen hose was clipped to the pilot's harness, plugged in and checked. Other things that needed to be checked included various services such as the gun heaters, fuel tank controls and the setting of important instruments like the altimeter and, of course, not forgetting the instrument panel clock, which had to be synchronised with the pilot's watch.

On the *Guardian Angel,* the assistant crew chief loosened the wheel chocks and gave the confirmation signal to Dom. Most pilots preferred to start up hard on the chocks and then have them removed, but Dom preferred it this way, as it gave him confidence in his brakes and made sure the chocks didn't get jammed.

After completing his pre-start and making sure the brakes are firmly on, Dom shouts, "Clear," which Dick Ferra repeats in his bull-like bellow. The starter motor turns and the big Rolls-Royce Packard Merlin groans and bursts into life.

Dom follows the other fighters out, slowly weaving along the narrow taxiway with Pepperman and the other two pilots following right behind. On reaching the end of the dark tarmacked runway on which they will take off, Dom selects 10 degrees of take-off flaps which will help with today's heavy fuel load then turns smoothly onto the runway. Without a hitch, the other three fighters of Red Flight turn and fall in behind him. At 9:32, Red Leader and his wingman roar off, gradually picking up speed along the runway. They are heavy today but the forty-eight fighters of the group depart Linton Grange smoothly in noisy pairs every ten to fifteen seconds. Once comfortably airborne, they fly a half-circuit of the airfield, form up and roll out onto their required course.

Visibility, although not excellent, is good, and the patchy clouds that cover eastern England are easily cleared in the gradual climb. Red Leader glances over his shoulder and sees what he wants to see: the three other P-51s sitting there in exact formation, forming a perfect 'finger four'. As they climb at bang on 170 mph, the green and gold fields of the English countryside rapidly disappear in the soft summer haze. The Mustangs, Rolls-Royce Merlin engines working hard, are soon over the North Sea and making their way towards the coast of Holland. The pilots put their oxygen masks on at 8,000', and the life-giving gas starts to flow at 9,000'. The altimeters continue to gently wind on upwards, showing the gradual increase in height: 11,000', 12,000', 13,000'. The pilots use these last few minutes before they reach the enemy coast to run through any essential checks, like making sure their new K14 gun sight is switched on, set and working.

At 23,000' and with the coast of Holland quickly approaching, the group leader orders 'battle formation', and the sleek fighters spread out so that they can cover a far wider area. The group, now at 25,000', passes over Walcheren Island and then, in a predetermined manoeuvre, turns slightly to the north to pass over the Zuider Zee whilst at the same time keeping well clear of the heavy flack installations around Texel Island. On and on they drone, mile after mile, with everybody keeping a sharp lookout for German fighters, as they are now well and truly in unfriendly territory. The radio is quiet; any communication now would be bad news. They are making for Dummer Lake in North West Germany but there is still quite a way to go. Dummer Lake is the point on the map where they are due to take over the escort relay from the shorter-range P-47s fighters who have covered the bombers for the first part of their mission.

Suddenly an excited voice yells, "Bogies dead ahead," the signal for unidentified aircraft... In the cockpits, the pilots' muscles tighten. Dom picks out the group of unidentified specks, directly in front, coming straight at them. They are fighters all right, but who are they? They have sharp pointed noses, but that means they could either be Me109s or friendly P-51s; only the next few seconds will tell. The Mustangs close up and prepare for combat. The mystery fighters look like they are going to fly straight through them. At the last second, someone calls in identification – the bogies are a new inexperienced but friendly P-51 group. Pilots' fingers move away from the gun-trigger switches and the friendly P-51 group fly over the top of the other Mustangs. The pilots start to relax a little. That had the making of a grade 'A' disaster.

Red 3's low sardonic voice quips, "Bunch of clown paddle feet," but the inexperienced pilots are lucky this time and streak on through, disappearing behind Dom's formation.

Someone else states the obvious: "Who needs enemies with friends like that?"

Dom chips in. "OK, settle down. Let's have RT silence and not squawk unless it's real important."

The group open out a little and for several more minutes continue on in serene fashion, everybody now scanning their little bit of private airspace. Suddenly another yell: "Bogies over there at about three o'clock, looks like they are turning into us!" Once again, the pilots of Dom's group tighten up and prepare for combat. Sharp noses again, Me109s or P-51s, who knows? Closer and closer they come, but they are prepared this time. Someone shouts, "Relax... same bunch of idiot monkeys."

To a chorus of cursing, the P-51s flash by again, underneath this time. An unknown voice makes a short quip over the radio. "Hope they're not going to make a habit of this!" In silence, the orderly flight continues through the clear blue sky; pretty soon, they should start to pick up the bombers as the big friends make their slow progress towards Magdeburg.

Another call: "Vapour trails dead ahead... looks like B-17s." The group leader guides the Mustangs, which are still 20 miles away, to the left of the bombers and confirms the premade plans for the three squadrons that make up the group. The four flights of four which make up Dom's squadron will fan out to the left and try and drive off any German fighters before they can get at the bombers. White Leader calls out that he has seen possible hostile bandits below and that Red Flight with Blue covering should go down and investigate. This is bad news for Red and Blue Flights, as they will have to drop their long-range external tanks, losing any remaining fuel in them. With the tanks still attached, manoeuvrability will be severely limited, so it is a chance they will have to take.

Dom gives the order: "Red Flight, drop tanks... Now," and the tanks fall away in pairs. He waits a few seconds to make sure all aeroplanes have successfully transferred onto internal fuel, then Red Flight gently stand their Mustangs on their starboard wing tips and scythe away to intercept the possible threat, with Blue Flight not far behind.

Dom glances over his shoulder to check on Pepperman. Good boy, he is right in place where he should be. Red Flight is still together and curves inwards under the bombers; a sudden shout: "There they are at nine o'clock, there must be fifty of the bastards. What's the plan?"

There is always a joker, and Red Flight has one in Gilburtson. "Well, there are only fifty plus of them and four of us, so how about we surround them!"

The situation is tense but Dom cannot resist a smile. "We'll go straight at them head-on and see if we can break them up." Red Flight followed by Blue Flight turn into the massed Me109s and Fw190s for a full-frontal attack. "Pepperman, stay with me. Red 3, pick a target on your side and I'll deal with this side." Dom has honed this tactic before and he times his manoeuvre to perfection. At the last minute, he swings the *Angel* into a hard right turn and pulls in behind one of the lead 190s. His K14 gun sight is working overtime, and the pips are coming into place nicely, working out the necessary deflection. He is now vulnerable to an attack from the rear but hopefully Pepperman and Blue Flight are covering him. The enemy fighters appear to be ignoring the American fighters and are going straight for the bombers. Friend and foe alike are now very close to the bombers, and the B-17 gunners are blazing away at everything in sight, as there is no time to work out who is who. The radio crackles continually with the sound of the air battle; there are whooping shouts of joyous relief as someone claims a victory but also screaming voices begging for help and assistance. Dom tries to temporarily blank out the noises from his brain, as he must focus on this 190 which is now filling his gun sight. He presses the trigger and the six 'point fives' spit out a hail of lead, which strike the 190 behind the cockpit, but it flies on. He kicks the rudder to get into a better position and fires again. This time, bits fly off and one of the landing gears of the 190 flops down. Over it goes onto its back and Dom notices the German pilot drop out of the cockpit as he takes to his chute. Dom pulls around, looking for a second target. "OK, Pepperman, close up." Dom sees a 109 lining up on a B-17 and turns hard to intercept him. With luck on his side, he will cut him off before he rakes the bomber. The angle is good; one last look behind to check that Pepperman is in place, but there is no Pepperman. Where the hell is he? There he is with a 190 hard on his tail. He racks the Mustang round and turns into the 190 as fast as he can. The German thinks better of it and breaks off the attack on his wingman. "Red 2, are you OK? Close up now." Pepperman clears his head and pulls in behind Red 1. The fight around the bombers is now intense; the sky is full of chutes; a B-17 is going down in a rolling fireball. Only one chute blossoms from the burning wreck where only a minute before ten young American men were safe and secure. Another is blown clean apart with the pieces floating down like falling autumn leaves.

Dom glances at his altimeter: 18,000 feet! They have lost quite a lot of altitude and have become separated from the other two Mustangs of Red Flight. He makes a radio call. "Red 3, your position," but there is no reply. Dom curses but what has happened is not abnormal. He makes a decision to head back towards the bombers whilst climbing as hard as he can with the throttle wide open. Glancing behind, he sees Pepperman is in place. Well, at least that part of the plan is working. All around him he sees enemy fighters, some individuals, some in pairs and others in larger groups. Buoyed on by the success of that last victory, Dom is tempted to make another attack on one of the singletons, but common sense tells him to gain more altitude, which will give him some protection and the upper hand, as the enemy fighters are concentrating on the bombers. Above him he sees a group of Fw190s chasing a lone Mustang. He pulls the stick hard back and the *Guardian Angel* climbs at what appears to be an impossible angle. The lead 190 is in the centre of his gun-sight glass but the range is too extreme. Never mind that; he pulls the trigger. If nothing else, the tracer will attract their attention and maybe make them think again. The tracers do their job and the four 190s nose down to take on the Mustangs, but the odds are bad, as Dom and Pepperman are on their own and climbing. He calls, "Hold your nerve, Pep, we are going straight through them." The two Mustangs are climbing fast; the diving enemy fighters are growing bigger and bigger as the two groups close on each other at a combined speed of nearly 700 MPH. The wing-leading edges of the 190s start flashing as they fire their wing guns, but the lead Mustang and his wingman are firing as well. "Atta boy, Pep, you've worked this out for yourself." Unbelievably, no one is hit on either side and the two Mustangs slice through the four Fw190s, causing them to split left and right.

The Mustangs continue climbing to get above the bombers, where they can do most good. Pepperman's attention is temporarily drawn to the clouds of black flak smudges that surround the bombers, but he is snapped out of it by Dom, who has identified a group of Mustangs heavily involved with the German fighters. He calls Pepperman. "OK, Red 2, let's join that party over there at three o'clock high."

As they climb back above the bomber stream, a Me109 dives straight down almost directly ahead of them. Dom rolls his Mustang on its back and pulls through to reverse direction, the classic split-S manoeuvre, but the 109 has got away. Pepperman is still there with him and has done well to anticipate what Dom had intended. During their dive, they spot three more 109s on the deck, heading east. Dom screws his Mustang round towards the last 109, with Pepperman following, but the dive is too steep and they have to pull out early. Dom's target whips to the left, whilst the leading 109 turns right and comes in below and behind Dom and begins firing up at him from 200 to 300 yards. Pepperman can't believe his luck; the attacking 109 pilot has not seen him and is now bang in his sights. He opens fire, landing several strikes on the German fighter. The 109 starts to billow black smoke, gives an uncontrolled shudder then goes out of control, crashing into the deck. At that altitude, the pilot doesn't stand a chance. The other two 109s then disappear, heading due east and away from the action.

The radio is still full of shouts and warnings. Some may be close; others may be not. Who can tell? It's more than likely that the enemy fighters have regrouped and must be hitting the bombers again. Dom and Pepperman close up and climb back into what appears to be an empty sky. How did that happen? One minute the sky was full of gyrating aeroplanes then they all disappear. Looking up and over to the north, they see the four Mustangs of Blue Flight who were supposed to have been covering them. Where the hell have they been?

Pepperman is struggling to take it all in. He has made his first victory. Automatically, he is following Dom's every move without really concentrating. Suddenly he is back in the moment as a voice is yelling at him. It is Blue 3, Bud Brooks, "Red 2, break left two six." Pepperman pulls back sharply and turns hard left, then he hears Brooks calmly and slowly saying, "OK, OK, I... got... him." Looking back, Pepperman glimpses Brooks following down a smoking Me109, with his wingman Freeman at Blue 4 still tightly in behind, protecting his tail. Realisation slowly hits Pepperman; Blue 3 and 4 have just saved his life.

Pepperman follows Dom in a climbing circle, where they are rejoined by Red 3 and Red 4. Blue Flight fall in with them; there is always protection in numbers. The eight Mustangs turn due west and head for home. Gilburtson as usual has something to say. "Nice shooting, guys. We're all here and heading home for a party."

But all is not what it should be. Brooks is flying erratically, though his speed seems OK. Engine oil blackens his fuselage. Is it his or has it come from the 109 he got? There is no way of telling. From a distance, there doesn't appear to be any damage to his plane. Blue Leader calls Brooks on the radio but incredibly the only reply he gets is a chuckle followed by the humming of an old music hall song. What in hell is happening? "Brooks, snap out of it. Get your ass into position now before you get separated."

They carry on in muted silence. Now Brooks drifts away from the formation; his corrections are slow and sluggish. Something is definitely wrong; he must be hurt. The other two members of Blue Flight try calling him on the radio, but the response is the same. A light bulb flashes in Blue Leader's brain: hypoxia, the classic symptoms of oxygen starvation. His system must have run out or failed. Blue Leader issues an urgent instruction to the other six Mustangs. "He's showing signs of O_2 starvation. Keep well clear, he will not be in full control of his kite. I'm going over to him and try and wake him up. If that works, I'll take him down to an altitude where he'll be OK."

Blue Leader gets closer to Brooks and, sure enough, the head of the almost incapacitated pilot is flopping around from side to side in the cockpit. Blue Leader tries some well-chosen words to get him to snap out of it, but there is no response. The only thing that is keeping the Mustang from falling out of the sky is its natural stability and some imbedded auto-response in Brooks, which is keeping the aeroplane flying more or less straight. Blue Leader calls Blue and Red Flights. "Stay clear. I'm going to try something. Keep your eyes open for hostiles." Their luck is in; the sky is clear. Blue Leader pulls behind and to the left of Brooks and pulls the gun trigger. The response is immediate; Brooks' head jerks to the left. Blue Leader is immediately talking. "Brooks, your oxygen is out. Follow me down." Brooks manages a nod and Blue Leader pulls in front of him and noses down with one last message to the other six. "See you guys later."

At 10,000 feet and with a haymaker of a headache, Brooks is now in full control of his Mustang. He tucks in behind Blue Leader and they make for home.

The remaining Mustangs head for base in a grim mood. The group have suffered some losses today, and now the extra concern over Blue Leader and Brooks. The transit over Germany to the North Sea coast is uneventful, though there's some flak over the Frisian Islands. Dom and Pepperman are the first aeroplanes back. Dom has a word with Dick Ferra about Blue Leader and Brooks. Dick will tell their respective crew chiefs not to expect them back for a while. It's a hard task but it's a job that has to be done, and with a little luck, they will turn up, if not back here at Linton Grange, maybe at one of the coastal airfields.

The pilots will be credited with six hours and ten minutes' mission time for the Magdeburg raid. Dom's total now stands at 251 hours, forty-five minutes, which will go towards the required 300 combat hours that will make him eligible for a thirty-day leave in the US. He and Pepperman will be credited with a victory each, which will now take Dom up to five and official 'Ace' status. During debrief, an orderly comes in with a message for the squadron lieutenant colonel, who shouts, "Listen up, we have just had a call come in from RAF Manston. They are both down and safe." The mood immediately lifts; there is going to be some serious celebrating tonight.

FOUR

FRIDAY NIGHT IS DANCE NIGHT

Dom's squadron is stood down for three days. They are tired but morale is high, even though the group suffered some losses on the Magdeburg raid. Time is a great healer and this three-day pass will help with that healing process. Already some of the pilots are making plans for a weekend in London. Dom, however, has his own plans; the city of Cambridge is not that far away but in the seven months he's been in England he has never made a visit. This would be the ideal time to do it. The three other pilots he bunks with are trying to convince him that he should come with them to London on Saturday but he will have none of it. The friendly discussion is interrupted by a message from the squadron boss asking Dom to drop in at his office. Dom wonders what this is all about. Has some past indiscretion finally caught up with him? He grabs his leather jacket and hat and makes his way over to the squadron office. He tries a friendly question on the CO's secretary but she has no idea what this is all about. She points to a chair and lets the CO know: "Captain D'Angelino is here," followed by, "OK, go on in."

*

Lt Colonel Bradley was leaning back in his chair smoking a Lucky Strike. "Come on in, Dom… Cigarette?"

Dom politely refused. "No, thanks, sir."

The lieutenant colonel continued. "Well, it appears that HQ have got to know about your exploits in becoming an 'Ace' and as usual, they want to make some mileage out of it. They love creating a bit of a morale boost for the folks back home."

Dom could see a problem coming here. "They are not going to send me home, are they, sir? I still have fifty hours to go and I would be real disappointed to not complete my tour."

Bradley smiled. "Nope, they are not going to do that. They're coming to you. Well, put it this way, they're going to send someone here to interview you."

Dom reflected on his plans for the weekend. "Will it be… fairly soon, sir, as I have made some plans… for the… er… weekend?"

Bradley waved Dom's concerns away. "Don't worry, it won't be until next week sometime… Meanwhile, I would like to personally thank you myself for what you are doing for the newer pilots on the squadron, especially for helping out young Pepperman yesterday. It's vitally important they don't have the confidence knocked out of them on their first mission. He has the makings of a first-class fighter pilot but as we all know, until you have a few missions under your belt, a little protection and a steady initial guiding hand are vital… I spoke to him after the mission and he freely admitted he had learned an awful lot, which is a good sign… Anyway… well done… it's appreciated."

This was getting a bit embarrassing and Dom just wanted to get out of the office. "I did no more than any of the other flight leaders would have done, sir."

Bradley nodded, paused and then added, "OK, Captain, that will be all… just one more thing… get yourself a dog… they always like pictures with a dog and of course make sure your crew chief is aware of what is happening. They will want to interview him and his team as well." Dom saluted, thanked the lieutenant colonel and left.

"Where am I going to get a dog? I don't even like dogs."

Gilburtson laughed. "Try Tech Sergeant Wilson, he's the go-to Mr Fix It. I'm sure he can rent you one."

Dave Zetterval immediately chipped in: "No, that's going to cost you money. Have a word with Brooksy. He's a happy boy at the moment, what with his close shave yesterday. He has a lovely-looking base-registered black Labrador he uses for rabbit shooting, follows him around like a shadow. I'm sure it would be your best friend for a piece of steak."

Gilburtson decided to move the conversation away from dogs. "Guys, we have three days off. Shouldn't we be talking about some friendly female company and not dogs? I'm sure the good captain here can sort out his own dog problems."

Zetterval was back in again. "Like we should listen to Gilburtson. Some of the dames he has dated were older than my mother."

Gilburtson took exception to this. "Some of them may not have been in their first flush of youth or beauty contest winners but so what? I'm a gentleman, and beauty, as my grandma would say, is only skin-deep."

One of the other pilots got their attention. "Talking of girls, are we all up for the show and dance at the Officers' Club tomorrow night?"

Gilburtson was straight in yet again. "I don't know… it'll be the same old same old bunch of hard-faced station WACs."

"Well, that's where you're wrong, Lieutenant. My spies tell me they have sent out invitations to truck in some local girls to give the show a kind of boost."

This was good news and even Dom said he would give it some serious consideration. "Who's the act for the show? Did your spies have the lowdown on that?"

"Of course, the station band will be there, and you have to agree they're pretty good. I think the main act is some Spanish singing dame."

"Interesting, where did they get her from?"

"Who cares, Spain, I guess. Are we all in?"

"You bet."

*

Rose Collins was never fond of this part of her working day, that is, the bus trip to Walden Green, where the company she worked for, Walden Adhesives, was located. It was only a twenty-minute ride but she hated sitting there with the other villagers, especially the boys, who all thought they were Clark Gable but had the brains of gnats. Luckily, her friend Liz, whom she had known all her life, had saved her a place next to her. Rose gratefully accepted the offer and sank into the worn green leather-covered seat. Liz, who also worked at the same place, locally known as 'The Glue Factory', struck up an immediate conversation about nothing at all, which Rose listened to with no great enthusiasm.

Rose and Liz had joined WA on the same day. For both of them, it had been their first job on leaving school, although at work they had gone in different directions. Liz had always been good with her hands and went off into production, whilst Rose had gone into the typing pool. Rose's teacher had observed the young lady's aptitude for handling the school's Imperial 'Good Companion' portable typewriter and had let her practise on it. In the end, it was that letter from Mrs Swain that got her the job. Although she would not admit it, as for her, it felt like a sign of weakness, Rose actually enjoyed typing. In fact, she loved machines in general and at home had often helped her older brothers out with jobs like removing and cleaning spark plugs from their old but much-valued V twin-powered Vincent Rapide motorbike. Payment was usually delivered in the form of a ride around the country lanes behind one of her brothers, something which was strictly forbidden by her parents.

Rose sat down at her desk. She knew exactly what the day would hold for her, as she was in the middle of typing up a huge report on a new improved resin glue the company was developing for the De Havilland DH98, something called a midge, or a mosquito. Anyway, whatever it was called, this new resin glue would make it even stronger.

The minutes moved by slowly and the chemistry in the report was extremely detailed, calling for her full concentration; Rose was really looking forward to that midmorning tea break. Bang on time, the tea lady arrived with the mobile tea urn and a meagre selection of buns, but what was this? Following close behind her was the department manager with a piece of printed paper in his hand. He addressed the girls of the typing pool:

"Ladies, I have some wonderful news for you. In appreciation of the work the company has done for the war effort, we have received an invitation on behalf of you ladies who work here... to attend a dance and show at the Linton Grange USAAF Flying Base Officers' Club tomorrow evening. Transport will be laid on and they promise to have you all home by 10:30." At this point, an excited buzz of approval ran through the typing pool. However, the excitement was not shared by the supervisor, Miss Straightstays, who showed a complete look of disgust. The manager continued...

"Those of you that are interested will find a list on the noticeboard. Please append your names to that list by the end of lunch break and I will let the base know who requires transport." With this, he turned and left the typing pool.

Miss Straightstays immediately vented her feelings. "Ladies, please let me remind you that these people are young American men, and those of you that have been to the cinema will know exactly what they are like."

A muffled voice from the back of the room was heard to say, "Oh dear, what are they like?"

Rose enjoyed her cuppa whilst thinking about the offer. "Sure I'll go, I'm big enough to look after myself, and it will be a chance to see another way of life. Only hope Mum and Dad don't cause problems."

*

At home that evening, Rose had a battle with her father, who didn't like the sound of dancing with young Americans, but her mother came to her aid. "Come on, Jack, give her a chance. She will be twenty in a few months' time and we were seriously courting at her age."

"But I wasn't some hillbilly from Tennessee or gangster from New York."

"No, you weren't, you were from over the border in Norfolk, which was even worse, and anyway, these will be officers, not enlisted men." At this point, Jack caved in and grudgingly gave his consent, along with a long list of do's and don'ts.

*

Friday end of work could not come quick enough for the girls in the typing pool, and Rose and her workmates were full of anticipation as they boarded their homebound buses. There wouldn't be much time to get ready, but Rose was well accomplished in the art of a quick change. She had got up early that morning to wash her hair and her mother had promised to get her meagre selection of clothes ready, so that she would definitely be there on time, along with the other girls from the village who had been invited. They were to be outside the post office ready for the pick-up at six thirty that evening.

The small group waited patiently for their transport and dead on time a green GMC 6x6 appeared, with a very polite driver who enquired if they were the ladies for the dance and show at Linton Grange. One by one, he checked off their names on a clipboard and helped them into the back of the covered transport with a pleasing line in encouragement. Someone had gone to a lot of trouble to try and improve the comfort of the hard slatted seats with layers of folded blankets. Once they were all in and settled, he announced that they had a couple more stops closer to the base to make, but the journey shouldn't take too long, wished them a pleasant journey and disappeared back into his cab. Being summer, there would be plenty of daylight saving, so the lack of lighting in the transport was not a problem. Someone remarked that, "This thing is like a cowboy covered wagon without the horses," which actually was pretty accurate, as the 6x6 was not exactly built for comfort.

At the air base gate, the truck was stopped by two military policemen resplendent in their white helmets and gloves. As the truck rolled to a stop, the driver called back through the cut-out in his cab.

"Relax, ladies, I will deal with the snowdrops," which caused a few giggles from the back. The driver jumped down from his cab and with a cheery word presented the clipboard to the policemen. The two MPs strolled around to the back of the truck and after a quick glance into the covered section sent them on their way with a, "Welcome to USAAF Base Linton Grange, ladies. We have been expecting you and you have a good time now."

Liz cupped her hand and whispered into Rose's ear, "What is it about Yanks? Whatever the situation, they always have the right line." Rose smiled; Liz was absolutely right!

The truck stopped outside the Officer's Club, which although built mainly from wood was to the girls' eyes quite an impressive-looking building of what appeared to be two storeys, that is, if the window layout was to be believed. They were met at the door by the Officers' Club president, who gave them a warm welcome and invited them in, explaining that they were a little early and that they were the first outside group to arrive but to be sure to make themselves comfortable. There were some officers grouped at the long bar to one side of a large hall area, who took a keen interest in their arrival, but apart from one lone wolf whistle and a couple of appreciative comments, did not make themselves known, but for them the night was young and there was still plenty of ice for the bourbon.

Looking around, it appeared the club was constructed with a large dance hall-like space in the centre surrounded by various small storage and kitchen areas. The second floor was, in fact, a mezzanine which ran along three of the four walls with a set of wide stairs leading up to it next to the entry door. The far end opposite the door was a stage, in front of which the station band was setting up. Around the three walls on both the lower floor and the mezzanine floor, small tables and chairs were set, some with pristine red and white gingham tablecloths, whilst others were blue and white. One of the girls remarked, "One of those would make a pretty dress for my sister," which brought some nervous laughter from her friends.

A friendly lieutenant shuffled over and invited them to find some tables, and when they were ready, to come on over to the bar. "I'm sure there will be plenty of gallant young men there who would love to buy you a drink."

Rose, who had somehow become the group's spokesman, said that she was sure they would take them up on their kind offer once they had found a seat. "By the way, we expected there to be many more people here."

The lieutenant reassured her. "Don't worry, ma'am, you're actually a little on the early side. Give it half an hour and this place will be jumping and you won't be able to see the floor."

The girls split up into several small groups, each looking for a table. Rose's group found a spot that offered a good view of the stage and dance floor and started chatting. Apparently, some of them had been practising what they thought were the latest dance fashions, being keen to make a good impression on their hosts. A tray of glasses and a large jug of punch arrived with a note saying, *Compliments of the Officers' Club*. The girls looked about for their benefactor but by now the building was starting to fill and it was impossible to see where it had come from.

The band struck up and after a few numbers, a couple took to the floor, closely followed by others, the officers all wearing their best 'Pinks and Greens' and their WAC partners in their special off-duty dresses of summer beige. Bang on 19:30, the president took to the stage and, after tapping the microphone to gain attention, announced that the dancing would shortly be getting into full swing, but before that, he would like to say, "On behalf of the Linton Grange OC, I am delighted to welcome all those local ladies who have given up their time to come along to brighten up our evening, so let's hear a good round of appreciation." The request was received with warm deafening applause.

He then went on, "The band will play for an hour, at which point there will be a short break, after which we proudly present for your entertainment all the way from Hollywood, USA, the fabulous singing sensation who is Miss Carmen Miranda, and after the floorshow, as is traditional, the band will play a few numbers so that we all go home with a warm bounce in our step." At this point, the band launched into a Glen Miller number and he left the stage. Rose's group were a little starstruck by it all, but the warming punch was having an effect and several feet were already tapping.

Red Flight entered the dance hall led by Gilburtson and Dave Zetterval, with Dom and Pepperman close behind.

"Late again."

"Not my fault if your mother never taught you how to use a smoothing iron."

"OK, boys, forget that and concentrate. We need to find some seats, we don't want to be propping up the bar all night."

"We're in luck, over there, next to the English girls," and with indecent haste, the four rushed across to bag the table just before a rival group from another squadron tried the same tactic.

"Bad luck, fellas, all's fair in love and war, remember… but look over there… another table, down by the stage." In one slick movement, Red Flight were seated, with their rivals walking away, looking confused but accepting defeat.

"Nice work." Gilburtson was in the seat closest to the girls and was already planning his next move.

"Good evening and welcome, ladies, could I ask where you are from?"

Liz was first to answer. "Oh, we are from a group of small villages near Cambridge on the Suffolk border. Most of us work at Walden Adhesives, don't know if you have ever heard of it?"

"Sorry, ladies, I didn't quite catch that, the band is very loud." Liz repeated her answer a little slower and louder.

"Sorry, this still isn't working. Would you mind if we pulled our table a little closer to yours?"

Liz, who had not worked out why she could hear them but they could not hear her, replied, "Of course not"… and yet another well-practised move had worked.

"Ladies, I'm sure you would like a little something to drink, but it would not be right to do that before introducing ourselves. This here is the good Captain Dom D'Angelino and we three lieutenants are Dave Zetterval, Pep Pepperman and I'm Victor – Vic to my friends – Gilburtson." Liz thanked them, introduced herself and invited the other girls to do the same.

One of the girls observed, "You seem to know each other really well. Are you all part of a team?"

"Yea, sort of, but people come and go. We are what is called a Flight of Four, and we also mess together, oh, and Pep here, he has only just joined us."

"So, Captain, you share accommodation with these three. I would have thought as a captain you would have your own room."

"Chance would be a fine thing, but I am working on it."

"Don't like our company, Captain?"

"I wouldn't say that, there are a lot worse!"

Gilburtson was in a hurry. He turned to Liz and asked her if she would like to dance, an offer which she readily accepted. They were closely followed onto the dance floor by Zetterval, Pepperman and the other two girls, leaving Rose and Dom alone at the table. Dom didn't quite know what to say. "I guess at this point I should ask you to dance, Miss Rose, but two things are bothering me. Number one, my dancing skills are pretty limited, and I'm not sure if I could manage this swing thing they are doing, and the second is, shouldn't we sit here and hang onto the table? This place is getting really packed." Rose smiled her agreement and leant forward to hold his hand.

"Don't worry, I'm no Ginger Rogers either. We'll wait until they play something slower."

"I don't believe that. An attractive lady like you must be the belle of the ball at your local village dances."

"Ah, you don't have much idea about 1944 English village life, do you?"

"Yea, well, you're probably correct about that. You're one of the first local girls I have ever spoken to. I've been to London with the boys a couple of times but quite honestly some of those London ladies scare me to death. They seem to think we have pockets full of dollars and nylon stockings."

"Oh, nylons, what are they!" Dom laughed.

"Yea, I guess most Yanks have no idea what you Brits have been through in the last four years." Rose really liked this American. He was not only good-looking but he was polite, softly spoken and obviously very intelligent.

"Well, that's very kind of you to appreciate our position. I just hope that, now the big invasion is well underway, this whole horrible war will come to an early end – but getting back to what you said, you're absolutely right, of course, about our shortages. See that dress Liz is wearing, that started out life as a set of curtains – that is drapes, I think you call them – and this dark trim around the hem of my dress, although he doesn't know it yet, that was part of my older brother's confirmation suit."

"Wow, won't he be a little upset when he finds out?"

"Probably, but as he is a Lancaster rear gunner flying night missions out of Lincolnshire at the moment, he's got much bigger problems to worry about."

"I can appreciate that… do you worry about him?"

"Every day… but I'm so rude, I've talked about nothing but myself. How about you?"

"Well, you've probably guessed I'm a pilot, have been for nearly three years now." Dom went on to explain in simple terms what a group, a squadron and flight were and how the four boys at the table flew four P-51 Mustangs as a flight, even showing Rose with the use of drinking glasses how they flew as a 'finger four' formation.

"But your name sounds quite Italian. Have your family been in the States long?"

"Oh yes, I'm a third-generation American from New York State."

"New York, wow, how exciting is that!"

"Well, actually not as exciting as my present-day job here in England."

"I can believe that, but I guess here tonight you are looking to relax."

"Well, that's certainly true, but you're never far away from it."

Rose was really enjoying this different, interesting conversation and just plucked something out of the blue.

"I think I know what a P-51 Mustang is. Do you fly those beautiful shiny blue and silver ones we sometimes see over the village?"

"No, unfortunately not, they belong to the 352nd up at Bodney. They're one of the top outfits, why do you ask?"

"Well, I had a close encounter with one a few days ago. It came over so low when I was up on Water Tower Hill, I literally had to throw myself to the ground."

Dom put his head in his hands and slowly said, "Exactly… which day was this?"

"Well, it must have been a weekend, as I wasn't at work."

"I don't suppose he came back and gave you a wave, did he?"

Rose was taken aback. "How did you know that?" But then the light dawned… "It was you… it was you, wasn't it? But it couldn't have been, it was blue and silver." Dom explained the whole story to Rose, who, far from being angry, was absolutely thrilled… Was this some kind of omen?

The band leader was at the microphone.

"Well, ladies and gents, we're going to change down a gear and slacken the pace a little, give some of the old-timers a chance to show off their ballroom-dancing skills." The band broke into *Good Night Sweetheart* and before he knew what was happening, Dom found himself being towed onto the dancefloor and, guess what, both were pleasantly surprised to find that the other was actually quite a good ballroom dancer.

"You're hiding your light under a bushel, Captain. You are quite a dancer."

"Please don't call me Captain. I get enough of that from those three – Dom or Don is fine, I answer to both."

"Well, I'm just plain Rose Collins."

"Plain you are not, Miss Rose. God, that sounded corny… In my defence, Rosalina was my grandmother's name. She was always called Rose." The band finished the number they were playing and went straight into *The Very Thought of You*.

"Why, another Al Bowlly song! The band must have known Linton Grange was about to be invaded by English girls."

"Sure thing, they will have definitely done their homework. Do you know, none of them are professional musicians, all serving airmen, to a man."

"Impressive, such dedication!" Rose closed her eyes and let herself get lost in the music. By the end, she was unselfconsciously resting her head on his shoulder. Snapping out of her temporary trance, she was back in the moment.

"Well, I could do with a drink. Back to the table?" Rose could sense the other girls' eyes looking at her but frankly she didn't care. This was more fun than she had had in a long while. The band leader came up to the microphone again.

"Ladies and gents, we have had a request for the Bob Hope and Bing Crosby number *Road to Morocco,* and not only that, something special to go with it, which I have to say some of the OC Club dance regulars will have seen before, but for our visitors... well, what can I say."

Dom had his head in his hands. "They said they wouldn't do this again, but a couple of beers and here we go."

Gilburtson and Zetterval were on the stage. Rose was intrigued. "What are they doing?"

"Don't worry, if it's what I think it is... it will be fairly self-explanatory." Gilburtson and Zetterval did a respectable impersonation of Hope and Crosby hoofing along to the old road movie number – which the visitors appeared to appreciate – took the applause and returned to their beaming admiring dance partners. Rose turned to Dom.

"Is there no limit to the talents of American airmen?"

"Well, that's one way of putting it, but hey, the floor show will be starting in a few minutes. I think we should squeeze in another dance."

The Officers' Club president came to the microphone once more.

"Ladies and gents, the OC Club of Linton Grange proudly presents for your entertainment the one and only...

Carmen Miranda." A person who obviously was not Carmen Miranda took to the dancefloor! She wore an extravagantly brightly coloured gown with a deep, revealing neckline. Finely balanced on her head was an extravagant decoration, which appeared to include the entire fruit and flower world. The dances were a perfect imitation of the real thing, being both extremely energetic but also provocative. The English girls were transfixed, many of them not knowing what to make of it. However, a few words of explanation from a lieutenant at the table next to them turned worried looks into broad grins.

After the performance, a lieutenant colonel from headquarters staff made a serious attempt to get more acquainted with Carmen but received a serious rebuff. Many of the OC members knew the truth, that this was not a lady at all but a young airman from another outfit. When the lieutenant colonel, who'd consumed a considerable amount of bourbon, had pressed his luck as far as the performer could stand it, he was, much to his great surprise and embarrassment, told the truth about the disguise. A look of complete horror spread across his face and he fled back to the bar. However, he eventually recovered his wits, took it all in good spirits and laughed it off. Rose turned to Dom again.

"Well, that was fun." Dom didn't quite know what to say.

"Believe you me, I didn't see that coming, and I'm sure Vic and the others didn't know either."

The other three nodded in agreement as Liz piped up, "Well, I thought he was great!"

The band were now playing the going-home waltzes, and couples were taking to the floor. Turning to Rose again, Dom suggested, "How about one final dance?"

Rose did not need any convincing and quickly led Dom onto the rapidly filling dance floor. As they navigated around the crowded floor, conversation flowed freely between them and Rose was feeling bold but... she was beaten to it by Dom. "Rose, could I see you again? Tonight has been so much fun and we really seem to hit it off."

"Well, let me see, but what would I say to my local boyfriend?" Dom's face dropped but then he saw the wicked smile on her face.

"I'm going to visit Cambridge tomorrow for the first time. I could really do with a knowledgeable guide. What do you say? I might even run to lunch."

"I'll have to check my diary but I think I'm free."

"OK, it's a date, but where shall we meet up? I don't know Cambridge at all."

"Well, the railway station is easy for me to get to. So how about there at eleven o'clock?"

"Suits me, I might even call in some favours and get a lift in with one of the provision trucks on one of their morning runs."

The final call was made for all the visiting ladies to please make their way out to the waiting transport. Without thinking, she pulled him to her and kissed his cheek.

"See you tomorrow," and she was gone.

FIVE

CAMBRIDGE

Captain Dom D'Angelino was at Cambridge station with an hour to spare and spent the time exploring the nearby streets, making sure he did not venture too far from the station and get lost. The few motorised vehicles he saw appeared to be military or public-transport types, and as far as he could make out, most people walked or rode bicycles, both of which seemed to lend themselves to the narrow and winding streets. He ventured down to the end of Station Road and turned right onto a much broader thoroughfare and, working on the theory that if you keep turning right you end up back where you started from, stumbled accidently upon a large open green area which was completely hidden from the main road. Some form of sporting match was about to start, which he assumed was the English game of cricket. Intrigued, he stopped to watch the players, all immaculately dressed in white, slowly go about their game. A nearby friendly bystander tried to explain what was going on but whichever way he looked at it, the rules seemed complicated and the amount of action minimal. Glancing at his watch, he bade farewell to his cricketing friend and retraced his steps back to where he had started.

He was back at the station with fifteen minutes to spare and suffered a moment of panic when he realised that Rose had not confirmed if she would be arriving by train or bus, which was further compounded by the fact he could see further down the street the occasional bus arriving and departing from a nearby stop. No, absolutely not... From what little he knew of Rose, if she said station, that's what she meant. Armed with a platform ticket, he marched onto the platform, eyes peeled, and was met with what appeared to be an almost deserted station. A uniformed rail employee was waiting with a sack barrow, so something must be due in. The London North Eastern Railway N7 0-6-2 tank engine and its load of three ancient Victorian-looking carriages came to a breathless, puffing halt in front of him. Why was everything in this town half-size?

Rose stepped down from the carriage with all the poise she could muster, but it was quite a drop and she was not used to the borrowed heeled court shoes she was wearing. Nevertheless, she was quite pleased with her effort. Dressed in her best grey skirt and a short-sleeved white blouse, topped off with a large red and light blue printed headscarf draped about her neck and shoulders, she felt like something out of a Donna Reed movie. Dom came running towards her, resplendent in his No1 uniform.

"You look a million dollars."

"You don't look so bad yourself, Captain." Dom went to put his arm around her but then thought better of it. After all, he had only met her last night.

"Have you been waiting long?"

"No, not really. I have had a quick look around but today I'm entirely in your hands. How long have we got?"

"Well, my last train back is at five thirty, how about you?"

"Won't be a problem, we have regular transport picking up new arrivals from most trains, so don't worry about me." Rose asked what he would like to see first, to which he replied that maybe they could start with the university. Rose smiled and replied that Cambridge University was in fact made up of a number of colleges, thirty-five to be precise, and each one had its own separate identity, such as Queen's College, Trinity College, St John's, and so on, and it might be easier if she just took him to the places she knew well. Dom readily agreed and they set off towards the city centre, admiring the fine old Gothic architecture along the way, some of which dated back to the thirteenth century. Dom was intrigued by some of the centuries-old ancient pubs they passed, each one with its brightly painted sign, and on this warm sunny day he was sorely tempted to suggest they enter and try some of their refreshment, but he managed to resist the call. As they walked along, Rose explained that the university owned most of the land in Cambridge and for them the foolishness of what was called progress was in no way acceptable, so he mustn't expect too much modernisation.

A succession of streets took them to a crossroads, on one of the corners of which there was a fine tall church that boasted both a tower and a spire.

"This church is called the Church of Our Lady of the Assumption and the English Martyrs, but it's a bit of a mouthful so everyone just calls it the Catholic Church, and although it looks ancient, it's only about fifty years old."

"Could have fooled me." At the crossroads, Rose took them down Lensfield Road making towards the 'Backs', but Dom, who was intrigued by any road in the middle of a city that was called Tennis Court Road, insisted on going down it. This required crossing the wide road and although there was little or no traffic, he offered his arm, which she gladly accepted. Rose was busy pointing out various landmarks as they made their way along the narrow street with its long, high three-storey buildings and miniscule pavements. Their journey took them past Downing College, Pembroke College and the delightfully named Corpus Christi College, Rose having to virtually tear him away from the Bowes & Bowes bookshop and a second-hand jazz record stall. Having got to the Silver Street Bridge, they rested, leaning on the railings and taking in the view of Silk's 'Punting Hire and Boatyard', which proudly displayed a sign saying, *Established in 1912*.

"I guess in peacetime this place was really buzzing."

"Do you know what, although I must have crossed this bridge a hundred times, I have never been punting. I've always assumed that the punts were reserved for university types. They seem to have this strange tradition that the freshman students punt the senior students about. Part of our class system, I suppose."

"Well, that's all going to change this afternoon, Miss Rose, because I'm going to take you punting down that river. How about that!"

"Well, suits me. Will I need a parasol to keep the sun off my delicate skin?"

"Is this the same young lady who, just like a latter-day sweet singing Greek siren, tried to entice a young airman to fly into a water tower in the same way those sirens of old would have enticed sailors onto the rocks?"

At this, Rose dissolved into a fit of giggles but quickly pulled herself together. "We must get going if you want to see the 'Backs' before lunch."

"Lead on, ma'am. Strange thing, you know, if I was naming some beauty spot, I would probably call it the front rather than the back."

"Very funny, Captain. It's because it's the land behind the colleges. Looks like beauty will be totally wasted on you."

"Oh dear, our first fight." Again, she burst into laughter and this time pulled his arm towards her as they stepped out onto the grass on the far side of the river.

Arm in arm, they strolled along the grassy weeping willow-shaded banks of the River Cam from which Cambridge gets its name. On the far side of the river, which could be crossed at various points by quaint little bridges of stone or wood, large trees shaded the green lawns and field pastures which led up to the backs of the magnificent college buildings. Incredibly, the occasional cow could be seen munching away at the lush green grass.

"Some farmer must be looking for them."

"Oh no, cattle on the Backs is quite normal, probably goes back to times gone by when they held country fairs here."

"This really is a strange town. One minute you are walking next to buildings designed by Sir Christopher Wren, did I get that right? And then you're in beautiful English countryside." Rose just smiled as they continued walking, but the pair came to an abrupt halt when the sight of King's College Chapel came into view.

"Rose, can we just sit here for a while? This is one of the most beautiful sights I have seen since being here in England." He took off his cap and then his jacket, which he spread on the ground so that Rose could sit without marking her clothes. No words were needed as they both sat there enjoying this peaceful moment.

"Well, Captain, I guess we ought to make our way back to the centre if we are going to get some lunch."

"I see. You are going to hold me to my rash promise of lunch."

"Well, why not? Don't all Yanks have pockets stuffed full of dollars?"

"Ah, you remember what I said last night, but seriously, I will purchase the best lunch available but on one condition."

"Hmm, I see, and what's that?"

"You just stop calling me Captain."

"Why? Have you been promoted to Major?"

Dom laughed and replied, "I wish… No, please call me Dom or Don."

"OK, it's a deal, but we better get going before they close."

Dom put on his jacket and took her hand. "Do we go back the same way we came?"

"No, if we keep going and turn back over the river, that will be quicker." They had only gone 50 yards when their attention was taken by the constant ringing of a bicycle bell. Turning round, they were confronted by a young lad on a delivery bike, waving furiously and shouting, "Stop." Dismounting from his delivery bicycle, which bore a large advertisement for the Dorothy Café and Ballroom, the breathless boy, who looked no more than fifteen, proudly reached into his delivery basket and pulled out Dom's peaked cap.

"You left it on the grass, sir. I thought you would need it."

"Well, thank you, I really appreciate your honesty. Can I reward you in any way?"

"Oh no, sir, what you're doing up there is reward enough. I'll be doing my bit soon. I'm off to join the Navy in a few weeks' time," and with that, he remounted his bicycle and disappeared into the distance.

They took an enjoyable lunch at a Corner House restaurant in Petty Cury, where Dom was intrigued by the rules and regulations, such as: three courses only, if you have fish you can't have meat, and the maximum total cost of a meal is 5/-. Dom called for the bill from the delightfully dressed waitress, who Rose explained was known as a Nippy, paid up and set off back towards the River Cam, taking a small detour to stop at the beautiful Trinity College entrance, where Dom remarked. "My college was certainly nothing like this!" to which Rose replied with her tongue firmly in her cheek, "Nor mine."

The Silk's boatman was not being very co-operative. "To be honest, sir, I think a row boat would be more suitable. Most American servicemen are more comfortable in one of those, and punting is a skill which takes some learning. Lord, I would hate for you to fall in and ruin that lovely uniform of yours." Rose was into the fray immediately.

"That's ridiculous. The captain here flies P-51 fighters at God knows what speed and at heights you couldn't imagine. How could punting be a problem?"

"Well, if you put it like that, ma'am, but I will need a deposit both for the punt and the pole."

"OK, no problem. How much?"

"One extra pound, sir, for each." Dom paid and, after getting Rose comfortably seated in the bow with a backrest and cushion, made his first attempt at propelling the punt and promptly nearly fell in.

"Take small steps, sir, don't be too ambitious. It will come with time, and don't try going faster until you're in full control." This seemed like good common sense to Dom and they set off upriver at a modest rate, with the boatman still calling out his advice.

"Don't get trapped between two boats, and watch the current doesn't sweep you downriver." Dom did not dare look back; he was too busy trying to steer and propel at the same time.

After fifteen minutes of a fairly sharp learning curve, he felt more in control and decided to make for a shady, secluded bank on the far side of the river. Strangely, Rose had been silent throughout the journey and he wondered what was up. Was she as scared as he was? They gently nudged the tree-lined bank and came to rest. Here, Dom tied the punt to a stout post. Rose nervously relaxed her grip on the gunwales. He made his way towards the bow and politely requested if there was any room for him to sit next to her. A request to which Rose readily agreed.

"This is lovely, although the journey was a bit scary." Dom laughed and sat beside her making small talk, which seemed to relax her.

"Dom, you never talk about flying and fighting, why do you do it? Is it because you have to or because you like it?"

"Well, I certainly love flying, there is no doubt about that, and as for fighting, the way I see it, we are there to protect the bombers, and the sooner they complete their job, the sooner this nightmare is over."

"But how do you feel when you blow some young German to pieces at 20,000 feet?"

Dom paused, staring at the blue sky, and then replied.

"When you're air fighting, you don't see the enemy as another pilot in a Me109 or whatever. You just see a cross-shaped metal box that is trying its best not only to kill you but also shoot down the bombers, those same bombers that from the other pilot's perspective are trying to destroy his country and family. I guess if I were him, I would do the exact same thing. It's not like the last war where pilots were supposed to be chivalrous knights of the air. It's definitely kill or be killed. If you are asking me, do I lie in bed at night asking myself what have I done, the answer is no. I just see it as a job to be done and if I didn't, I couldn't do it."

"Sorry, Dom, I don't want to make you feel bad. It's just so hard for a country girl like me to grasp the concept, but you have explained it so well and without doubt it's a hard job that must be done, just like my brother's."

"Don't worry, I have had a similar conversation with many people, including my own mother and sister... but right now, I'm miles away from all of that, sitting in this punt with a beautiful girl."

"What a smooth operator you are, Captain Dom D'Angelino."

"Ah, ah, remember your promise, Rose Collins."

"Just one more question, please."

"Fire away."

"As a child, for me, it was church three times on a Sunday, singing in the choir with my brothers. We were brought up to fear and respect religion, although, in the end, I actually came to my own conclusions."

"Oh and what is that?"

"Please, a lady must have some secrets, but how about you?"

"Nice answer, Miss Collins, but you know, when I first started flying escort missions, I noticed that some pilots would attend a short religious service with the chaplain straight after a mission briefing. That is just before they went out to the planes, but then I became aware of two things. For starters, none of our flight leaders ever attended the service, and second, many of those who attended never came back, so I too came to my own conclusions… but this conversation is getting much too serious."

Rose smiled at him, flashing her big blue eyes with a questioning look, and Dom, having no answer to that question, paused and then without thinking pulled her to him and kissed her hard on the lips.

A passing rowboat full of far too many enlisted men was now only a short distance away. One of them shouted out, "Go to it, Captain." This really riled Dom, who gave the miscreants a more-than-firm reprimand, reminding them who they were and that if they did not look out they would be swimming home. Fearing further action, they rapidly departed.

Time was flying and they still had to return the punt and get Rose back to the station. After half walking, half running, the station was reached with five minutes to spare. "Rose, I have a hell of a problem. Unless I'm on a pass, like now, I have no way of knowing when I have time off, things change by the hour, so I don't know when I can see you again. Could I have your phone number?"

Rose chuckled. "Phone number! Don't talk of phone numbers, we have only just got electricity in the village. Private phones are very rare, and personal calls at work are strictly forbidden."

Dom looked perplexed. "So when can we meet again?"

"Tell you what, I will give you my address. You can write or maybe just turn up. I don't know what my dad will make of it, but we will just have to jump off that bridge when we come to it." Rose was still scribbling her address on a scrap of paper when the guard blew his whistle and, thrusting the paper into his hand, she made her seat with seconds to spare. In a cloud of steam the train pulled out, leaving Dom a lonely figure on the platform.

SIX

BENTLEY DOES HIS DUTY

Monday morning arrived and Dom was not flying, as the colonel had arranged for the HQ photography section and liaison officer to visit at 10:00 hrs. The previous evening, Lt Brooks had introduced him to Bentley, his trusted black Labrador.

"Dom, this is Bentley, man's best friend."

"Good to meet you, Bentley. Are you really friendly?"

"Oh, he is friendly, all right, aren't you, boy? But there is a key to his long-lasting friendship." Brooks produced a handful of crushed dog biscuits from his pocket, which immediately got Bentley's full attention.

"I see the way it goes, the hand that feeds you and all that." Brooks laughed. "But, Brooksy, he's a fine dog. How did you come by him? He's no ugly stray mutt like some that have been adopted around here."

"Won him at a poker game from an HQ major who thought he could play poker."

"Ouch, that's a bit cruel, isn't it?"

"Not really, he had two others."

"How did he come by the name Bentley?"

"I guess he was not quite up to the level of his brother and sister."

"And who were they?"

"Oh, Daimler and Rolls, of course."

Dom laughed but Bentley put on one of his hurt looks; it was almost as if he had heard the story before. "You'll do, Bentley," he said, patting the dog. "You flying tomorrow, Brooksy?"

"Sure am but the word on the street is it's just a milk run to Northern France and we should be back for lunch." Brooks handed over Bentley's crushed biscuits and headed out the door. Bentley made no attempt to follow; his eyes were firmly fixed on the brown bag in Dom's hand.

Dom met the photographer and the liaison officer at the *Guardian Angel,* which Dick Ferra and his team had polished to within an inch of her life. The *Angel* looked magnificent but strangely lonely, sitting there on her own with most of her friends in the air 200 miles away. Bentley played his part to perfection and appeared completely unfazed by the whole thing. The HQ team tried to squeeze as much personal information as they could out of Dom, but this was something he jealously protected, giving them just enough to keep them happy. Questions like, 'Has Bentley ever gone flying with you?' were given short shrift, with Dom holding firm and keeping to the official line. Dick Ferra and his team appeared to be enjoying it all, however, and when the attention shifted onto them, Dom was quite happy to take a back seat.

The team finished the interviews, and it was whilst they were packing up that Dom asked a question. "The boys and I would really appreciate any spare prints you may make, you know, for family and our girls back home." The photographer indicated that it wouldn't be a problem, clambered into the Jeep with the rest of the crew and departed. Dom walked back across the grass and checked with Operations when the squadron was due back. It would be fitting for Bentley to be there to greet Brooks on his return.

At the appointed time, Dom made his way back to dispersal with Bentley trotting close behind. A quick search along the line found Brooks' crew chief and assistant sitting on the grass, waiting patiently in silence; this was always a tense time. Dom greeted them and took his place on the grass with Bentley, who was on the lookout for the occasional hare that could be seen in the distance, and when he saw one, he would utter a quiet stifled bark in his throat which made his jowls quiver with excitement. This had been a relatively small mission with just one squadron from the 8th helping out in escorting some 9th Air Force B-26 Marauders over France.

The first flight arrived back as a foursome but from then on the Mustangs were coming back in ones and twos, which indicated there had been some action. Brooks' crew chief was looking worried when ten had been counted in, but there was still plenty of time.

Things reached a peak of tension when Blue 4, Brooks' wingman, landed and pulled into the bay next to where the now-standing group were waiting. Having completed everything needed on his Mustang and, after an explanatory word with his own crew, a serious-faced Blue 4 came across.

"Last I saw of him he was going down for one last strafing run just behind the front line. I was low on fuel so he told me to head for home... Sorry, guys." With this, he turned and walked towards the waiting Jeep. The mechanics, obviously distressed, walked over to the crew of Blue 4, leaving Dom a lonely figure, with Bentley sat on his haunches still staring into the distance. Dom turned and slipped the leash through Bentley's collar, telling him there was nothing more they could do, but he was brought up short with a jolt by Bentley on his first step, who was going nowhere, still holding his gaze along the runway at the horizon. Dom thought of remonstrating with the dog but instead looked at where the dog was staring. Was that something in the distance on a very flat approach? As he tried to decide, a cheer went up along the line. Others had noticed too; it was the last Mustang, obviously with some sort of hydraulic problem, doing a fast and flat flapless landing. As they watched, Brooks performed a near faultless but very long flat approach and landing, bringing the Mustang to a halt right at the end of the runway. The emergency vehicles were all around it but were not needed; the tow tractor had it back on the designated pan in fifteen minutes.

Brooks jumped out and greeted Bentley with some hugging slaps and, turning to Dom, "What... why all the commotion? I knew I may have landing problems so I let the others go first. I didn't want to foul up the runway and cause them a load of hassle." Dom just shook his hand and, wearing a relieved smile, thanked him for the loan of Bentley and walked away to get some rest; he was flying the next day.

*

Dom taxied the *Guardian Angel* back onto the hardstanding, with Pepperman not far behind. Today, the day after Brooks' heroics, had been a complete waste of time. They were just approaching the Dutch coast when they had been recalled; the bomber mission had been scrubbed for bad weather over Germany. Still, the weather here in England was near perfect and the rest of the day would be his. Thoughts of Rose had been in his head all the way back across the North Sea, and he had made up his mind to borrow a Jeep and drive over and see her tonight. If her father threw him out, so be it.

Lintock village was only 13 miles away and even if he did not know the roads, he had a tongue in his head to ask directions, and he should be there in thirty minutes. He formulated a plan: must not arrive too early, they may still be eating their evening meal, and some sort of small gift would be appropriate. He had heard that food rationing was tight in England so maybe some cans of 'C' rations would help. Who was that go-to sergeant that Gilburtson had told him about?

Armed with several assorted cans of what the military laughingly called cream, chipped meat, beef and ham, etc., plus a can of tinned fruit, he set off for Lintock, which was harder to find than he thought, mainly due to the fact that many road signs had been removed or painted out as part of the early war anti-invasion precautions. Once he found Lintock, navigation was easy, as it really looked to be a one-street village. He stopped on the street just a few yards from the garden gate leading up to the small but neat country cottage which bore the name Rose had given him.

Dom collected his small parcel of tins from the back of the Jeep, straightened his jacket and opened the small wooden gate. As he walked up the path, he noticed that what had obviously once been a small grassed lawn area now contained neat rows of vegetables, with green beans on his right and a variety of onions, carrots and cabbages on his left. A sign of the hard present times, he guessed.

Well, this was it, now or never, and taking a deep breath he raised the small-cast iron fox's head door knocker and gave it a short rattle, praying that it wouldn't be Rose's father who came to the door. Hearing movement inside, he stepped back in anticipation. It was Rose's mother who was standing there looking somewhat mystified. "Can I help you, young man?"

Dom had his opening lines well rehearsed, but those words had flown away.

Stumbling over what to say, he managed to get out... "I was wondering if... this would be where Miss Rose Collins lives. We met up a few days ago and as I was in the area I thought I would maybe call in on her."

Jane Collins hesitated but her face brightened and she was quick to reply.

"You must be... Donald. Rose has talked about nothing else but you these last few days."

"Well, actually, my name is Domenico. Domenico D'Angelino, to be precise, but I answer to Dom or Don. I don't mind either."

"Well, please come in. Rose is up in her room at the moment, but I will go and get her. Meanwhile, please take a seat in our sitting room. Rose's dad is in there but he will have his head buried in the weekly newspaper if I know him."

Jane Collins showed him in and disappeared up the stairs, leaving Dom sitting there with the parcel of tins on his lap and Rose's father, Jack, sitting on the other side of the room, invisible behind the weekly broadsheet.

Mrs Collins appeared at the door. "Rose will be down shortly. Can I interest you in a cup of tea?" Jack Collins slowly lowered his newspaper, not looking best pleased, they had already had their tea ration for today, but he said nothing, raised his newspaper again and continued reading. Dom wondered if he should try and make conversation or wait for Rose to appear. Mercifully, she appeared before he had to make that decision. "Dom, how lovely to see you, this is so unexpected. How did you get the time off?" Dom explained in simple terms what had happened and asked Rose if the family could use any of these, handing her the parcel, which she quickly gave to her mother.

"Dad, you are being very rude, we have a guest. This is Dom, the young man I told you about."

"I know who he is, all right, in that fancy uniform."

Rose's anger was rising. "Why do you have to spoil everything? Dom is the perfect gentleman and if you bothered to talk to him you would know that."

Jack Collins might be abrupt but he did not want to appear ignorant. "Please accept my apologies, but my experience of Americans has not been good. You could say I am a little biased."

"I'm sorry to hear that, sir. What was that experience?"

"Well, I was in the last lot, served two years in the trenches in Northern France and when it was all over and we were on the boat, waiting to come home, a crowd of Yanks came on board, many of them sick with the Spanish flu. Well, it went through that ship like a dose of salts, I can tell you. Lost my best friend, Les Fothergill."

"Again, I'm sorry to hear that, but surely that was just an unfortunate accident."

"You might see it that way, son, but to me it was avoidable. Myself, I've had a weak chest ever since so I don't forget."

Dom was momentarily stumped for words but was rescued by Rose's mother, who came in declaring, "Thank you for the food you brought. It will make a lovely change to our normal diet."

"No problem, Mrs Collins, glad to be of help."

Jack Collins was still not finished. "What food is this?"

"Well, several tins of creamed chipped meat and some tinned fruit."

Jack Collins was chuckling but before he could speak, Rose's mother intervened. "Take no notice of him, Don. I know what he is going to say." Rose was looking baffled. Her mother hesitated but then went on, "Well, there is a certain lady in the village, a Mrs Queenie Sutton by name, who sells buckets of creamed chicken to the Officers' Club over at the American airbase behind Hadstock."

Dom shrugged his shoulders; he couldn't see a problem. "Creamed chicken is a great American favourite."

"Well, the trouble is, these chickens never had feathers. It's rabbit. Her poacher of a husband traps them, and to add insult to injury, she makes gloves out of the skins and sells them to the enlisted men."

Dom could not control his response. He just burst out laughing, adding, "Fine businesswoman, if you ask me." This seemed to break the ice and mollify Jack Collins a little, who then spent the time waiting for the tea to arrive, asking Dom civil questions, the replies to which he listened to attentively. Dom returned a question: "And how about you, Mr Collins, what do you do?"

"Well, if I could, I would be serving like my two sons, but as a head dairyman I'm in a reserved occupation and anyway with my chest they wouldn't have me."

"I know about Rose's brother, who is an air gunner in the RAF, but where does your other son serve?"

"Royal Navy, on Russian convoy escort Destroyers. We don't see much of him from one month to another."

"I know the feeling. I have not seen my folks for over seven months."

Jack Collins was about to ask if Dom had any brothers or sisters but was interrupted again by his wife with, "Tea is up," and they all trooped out to sit around the kitchen table. Rose was aching to get Dom all to herself and was quick to suggest that once they had finished the tea she could give him a quick tour of the village. Rose's mother was in a playful mood and chipped in, "What a good idea, it's a lovely evening and I could do with a breath of fresh air. Do you mind if I come with you?" Rose gave her a look which could kill but relaxed straight away when her mother added, "I'm only teasing. You young things get along and enjoy yourselves."

Rose knew that her mother would be watching from an upstairs window so until the cottage was well out of view she walked demurely beside Dom, not even holding his hand. However, as soon as they had started down the horse chestnut tree-lined, slight dog leg-shaped part of the main street, she stopped and turned towards him. For a moment, they just looked at each other but then, and they didn't know and didn't care who started it, found themselves in a passionate embrace. "Rose, you won't believe how much I have missed you, even to the point where I've found it hard to concentrate on my flying."

"Don't talk… just kiss me again." Dom just did what he was told, but Rose quickly decided that maybe they should show a little discretion, as this was a small village and net curtains would be twitching and tongues set wagging.

"Let's just walk on and go down to the river. It's beautiful down there at this time of the year." They turned down a narrow street with houses on either side which turned into a lane leading to the river.

"You know, I didn't even notice this street on the way in, drove right past it, but hey, look at that fantastic ancient plaster and wood-faced building. It's got to be Tudor, right?"

"Don't ask me, I've always known it as the Guildhall. It's a private house now." As they strolled on down the lane, Rose pointed out various places of interest, including the church and her old junior school. Ahead of them loomed a tall wooden building which dwarfed the small cottage next to it. "That's the mill. After harvest, when it's going full pelt, this whole area will be covered in yellow dust. As kids, we used to play in it. Probably didn't do us much good, thinking about it."

"I don't think it did you much harm, Rose Collins." Arm in arm, they walked on, following the footpath which wound its way along the riverbank until Rose decided they should cross over at the footbridge. Halfway across the bridge, they stopped and studied the water passing underneath. "We do seem to spend a lot of time on bridges."

"True, but do you know, as a kid back in the States, if ever I had problems or worries I would go to our local bridge and pretend to drop my worries in and watch the river wash them away."

"That's lovely, but a bit unfair on the river, don't you think?" Dom smiled and gave Rose a peck on the cheek as they continued on over to the cow pasture that ran down to the other side of the river. The evening sun was now getting low over the trees, so they found a sunny spot where they could still feel its warming rays. "This field is part of the dairy farm where Dad works. Most of the land further up the hill is poor pasture and only fit for wheat."

"Talking of your father, I don't think he likes me."

"Take no notice. I'm the youngest and also his only daughter, so he is very protective. And to be honest, I have never been the perfect daughter, been in a few scrapes, but you don't want to hear about them."

Dom just grinned and shook his shoulders before going on. "Rose, would you be free next Sunday? I have a rest day and I'd like to show you the base, sort of give you a better idea of what I do… Should I ask your parents' permission?"

"I'd love to or put it another way, try and stop me." Rose decided, maybe better not ask her parents. "Mum wouldn't mind but Dad could be a problem. You know how he can be a bit opinionated. I'll just tell them I'm spending the afternoon with Liz. She will cover for me if they ask questions."

Dom returned Rose to her home, where her mother was pottering about the front garden, obviously keeping a lookout, but before they got within earshot, Dom whispered in Rose's ear, "About Sunday, could you remember to wear pants?"

An alarmed Rose stopped, abruptly exclaiming, "What?" which led an embarrassed Dom to declare, "Sorry, sorry, I mean trousers or slacks. That's what you call them, isn't it?"

Rose burst into laughter. "For a moment, I thought you were making an improper suggestion," but by now they were at the gate, where they were greeted by Rose's smiling mother.

"Well, you two sound like you have been enjoying yourselves."

Dom said his goodbyes, reminding Rose to be ready at two o'clock, and jumped into the Jeep. In thirty minutes, it would be fully dark, so he really ought to be on his way.

SEVEN

OLD *WAR-WEARY*

Dick Ferra opened the side personnel door of the T2 and made his way to the far end of the hangar, behind him his friend Tech Sgt Griffin. "Well, there she is, what do you think?"

"Well, I wouldn't call her the best-looking P-51 I've ever seen, but I guess she cuts the mustard, better than the botched job it's rumoured they stuffed General Ike in. Whose idea was this?"

"It all started a couple of months ago with Woody Jensen the T/Sgt technical inspector for the 335th down at Debden. He put forward a request to convert an old war-weary B model into a two-seater so that some of the new pilots who had only trained on other types like P-40s could get some P-51 time in before going solo in the real thing."

"Makes sense, so you guys copied."

"We got to know about it from a couple of mechanics who got transferred up here from Debden. At the time, we had three severely damaged/beyond repair C models sitting at the back of the hangar, basically waiting for the scrap man's torch and just wasting space. Two of them had been involved in a taxiing accident where one had run into the back of the other, chewed up the ass end of one and smashed the nose of the offender, both of them way past redemption. The third one was just high on hours and missing an engine. Command had told us that we were about to receive D models, so the three of them were just left here, not worth any attempt at repair, I guess."

"So basically you made one useable airframe out of three."

"That's right, we took the engine out of the one with the chewed-up tail and put it in the one missing a donkey, that's old WW, *War-Weary* here. Next, we took the radio and internal tank out of her and fashioned a second seat and a Perspex hood using parts from the other two. The radio is a tight fit, but we managed to shoehorn it in under the rear fuselage decking."

"What did top brass think about it?"

"All for it. Most of the work was done by volunteers so it didn't cost a cent of tax payers' hard-earned money, plus we had some great backing from our squadron flight leaders. My line pilot, Captain Dom D'Angelino, took her up for her first test flight. The experts had worked out she would need some tail end ballast, so I volunteered to sit in the back, and off we went."

"And how does she perform?"

"Would you believe the pilots say she flies much the same as the original?"

"Cleared for aerobatics?"

"No, not yet. Due to the metal we have removed from

her back, some of her stressed skin strength may have been reduced but we have hopes."

"OK, I see that. Any other additional improvements?"

"Sure have, she is now the proud possessor of dual controls."

"Very impressive, wouldn't mind a flip in her myself."

"You'll have to join a long line. Believe me, there is no shortage of volunteers to look after her."

"I can believe that. Any chance of a look at the second seat position?"

"Of course, be my guest... To open the rear hood, you have to open the front side panel and reach back inside for the catches. It's a little tricky but you soon get the hang of it."

Griffin jumped on the port wing and soon had his head inside the second seat position. "Looks real neat, I see there are a few empty holes in the instrument panel."

Ferra came closer to the trailing edge. "Yes, the aim is to get a complete set so she can be flown from the front or back, but that'll involve a lot of new wiring so it may have to be done little by little. However, just this week we fitted an airspeed indicator and an altimeter to the rear panel, and in fact Captain Dom is going to give her a quick flip tomorrow to check that the accuracy of the front seat instruments hasn't been affected by the alterations. Meanwhile, I have to check that nothing leaks. Fancy giving me a hand?"

Griffin was keen to get involved and was quick with his reply. "Sure, I'll go and get the test rig," and so saying, he slid off the wing and set off towards the workshops on the far side of the hangar.

*

By Sunday morning, Dom had everything arranged down to the last detail, but he was not a natural rule breaker and he found that even just bending them a little made him feel uneasy. But, as Gilburtson would say, Uncle Sam wouldn't mind and anyway, we could all be dead by tomorrow. That was a little strong but as always there was an element of truth in it. The day was gin clear, ideal for what he had planned. The trip over to Lintock was mainly uneventful and much quicker now that he knew the way. The only hazard he faced was a large bunch of enlisted men on bikes who were using a slack Sunday to explore the local countryside. As he approached Lintock down the steep hill on which the water tower was located, he realised that there was something important that he had forgotten. Rose had said she was spending the day with Liz; how suspicious was it going to look if he just turned up at the front door? But there was no time to worry about that now. He stopped on the street in exactly the same spot he had parked in last time. There was a few minutes to spare before two o'clock, which would give him time to work something out. His heart leapt as Rose appeared at the gate and then sank when he noticed her mother was with her. Rose strolled to the Jeep, resplendent in a long straight pair of khaki pants. God, she looked terrific. "It's OK, Dad is at work and Mum won't tell."

"Your mom is something special, you know that? She's one in a million." They drove off slowly with her mother waving after them as they disappeared down the street. Rose gave him a friendly peck on the cheek and, leaning on his shoulder, put her arm around him. "Steady on, young lady, can't you see I'm concentrating on the road ahead?" Rose slowly took her arm away and leaned back in her seat, letting the warm rush of summer air blow through her long hair.

Dom pulled over and stopped the Jeep just before they reached the base. From the back he produced a pair of flight overalls and leather jacket. "Here, put these on over what you're wearing." This was exactly the kind of intrigue she enjoyed, so she followed his instructions without a fuss. "Now put my hat on and tuck your hair in under it." Finally, he produced a pair of Bausch and Lomb AN regulation sunglasses and said, "Pop these on, Rose."

Rose leaned across and looked in the rear-view mirror. "Why, if I didn't know the truth, I would really fancy this guy."

"Rose, stop fooling around and pay attention. We are going round to the maintenance gate. It'll be real slack there, as it's a weekend and there are no 'ops' on. There is only one policeman on duty and he knows I'm due back with another officer about now, so with a bit of luck, he will raise the boom when he sees us coming and we can drive straight through. Just look relaxed and stare straight ahead."

"Why all the cloak and dagger stuff?"

"I'll explain when we are inside."

The plan worked a treat and they were in. Once out of sight of the gate, Dom stopped and turned to Rose. "Rose, I must be completely nuts and my Air Corps career could end right here, but I'm going to take you flying in our two-seat P-51 Mustang."

"We're going to do what!"

"Go up for a quick flip. It's the only two-seater on the base and it's in need of a test flight. So basically I have a spare seat, are you game?"

"Me... fly in a US fighter airplane... am I dreaming? Well, yes, of course I will. Just one question, though. Dom, are you better at flying than you are at punting?"

Dom just laughed and continued. "When we get to the aeroplane, just remain in the Jeep until I call you over. I will have to distract my mechanic whilst I get you installed. OK?" Rose nodded her understanding and sat perfectly still.

War-Weary was sitting outside the T2 hangar, looking far from tired in her new group paint scheme. Dom jumped out of the Jeep and strolled over to his mechanic, who was sitting on the grass. "Hi, Tony, how are things?"

"Looking good, Captain. She is A1 with an hour's worth of gas in her. Will that be enough?"

"Sure will, we won't be gone much more than thirty minutes. Could you do me a small favour? I have left the flight-check manual I need on the flight office desk. It's labelled *Airspeed/RPM Charts for Still Air*. Oh and don't worry about things here. I will get the passenger installed."

"No problem, Cap," and off he strolled.

As he was walking away, Dom beckoned Rose to the aeroplane. "Up you get, young lady. I'll be round the other side to help you in." Dom quickly had the two canopies opened and Rose quickly had herself neatly in place in the rear seat.

"Oh, pretty tight fit," Dom laughed. "Just one thing, keep this flying helmet on and please don't touch anything." Rose gave her affirmative on the Girl Guide Honour, an organisation she was totally unfamiliar with.

By the time the mechanic was back, Dom had done his walk-round and was carrying out his cockpit checks. The second canopy was closed, so Rose was well hidden. "Thanks for that, Tony. We will do a standard start and be away. Don't hang around waiting for us to return. I'll make sure everything is where it should be and put the aeroplane to bed."

The mechanic loosened the chocks, pulled the prop through four blades and, stepping well back, shouted, "OK, Cap, ready when you are."

Dom went through the well-practised starting routine and, once the engine was purring evenly, gave the signal for the chocks to be removed. "How you doing back there, is everything OK?" Rose leaned forward and tapped him on the shoulder. "No, Rose, if you want to talk to me, please use that switch I showed you, because the engine will be real noisy."

Rose quickly had her microphone and intercom working. "I'm wasted as a typist, you know."

Dom laughed; that was so typical of her. "Here we go then. Last chance to pull out."

"No chance, Captain… take me to heaven."

Dom gave the thumbs-up to the mechanic and the Mustang moved out and started making its way slowly towards the end of the runway. The radio crackled in Dom's earphones. It was the tower. "Unidentified P-51, please state your intentions."

"Roger, Tower. This is *War-Weary* P-51. I will be conducting a thirty-minute air test to the south of the base."

"Understood, *War-Weary*. Hold when you reach the holding point and await further instructions."

"Roger, Tower, will do."

"OK, *War-Weary*, you are cleared onto the runway. Once you get a green from the runway controller's van, you are cleared for take-off."

"Roger that, Tower." Dom pulled onto the runway with his eyes firmly on the red and white chequered van. Rose sat motionless, mesmerised by the giant propeller which was beating in time with the Merlin engine. A green Aldiss light from the control van flashed. "Here we go then." The noise was almost unbearable as Dom advanced the throttle, and things started moving very quickly when he released the brakes. At first, Rose just stared blankly ahead, unable to take it all in, but scanning left and right she could just make out long rows of silver long-range drop tanks piled up in the distance and the T2 hangar as it receded in miniature. Slowly, the tail came up, the wheels bumped a couple of times and they were airborne and climbing away. Within seconds, Linton Grange was left well behind. Rose was absolutely enthralled; could this really be happening to her, Rose Collins, the typist from Lintock! But one thing she was sure of, she had never felt more alive than she did at this moment.

"Rose, try and sit back and relax. We're going to spend a few minutes gently climbing."

"No problem, your wish is my command." She spent the time trying, a little unsuccessfully, to identify villages on the ground as they passed below, but they all looked the same.

"OK, Rose, I have a little work to do and then we can have some fun."

"Don't mind me. I have plenty to look at back here."

"Good point. Actually, you can help me. See that large round gauge in the middle of the panel with numbers that start at 40?"

"You mean the one with the knob at the bottom?"

"No, that's the altimeter. That one shows our height."

"Good God, it's saying 5,000 feet."

"That's OK, quite normal… I mean the gauge next to it."

"Got it… Let me see… I make that 190 MPH."

"Pretty good, same as mine. I have to take a few readings and then you will have my full undivided attention. By the way, we're heading towards Saffron Walden. Isn't that where you work?" Suddenly the full map-like picture came into focus; she could even see Walden Adhesives.

Dom finished his instrument checks and was on the intercom again to Rose. "Anything you would like to see, madam?"

"I know this sounds childish but I would really like to get up close to that enormous cloud over there."

"He's called a towering cumulonimbus or in everyday language a thunderhead, home maybe of a thunderstorm. The smaller ones around its base are usually quite innocent, so we can have a closer look at one of those if you like."

"Yes, please." Dom rolled the Mustang towards the cloud formation.

"No problem. You know, Rose, when I first started flying, I always found clouds a little disappointing, especially when you get up close or inside one. The best angle is looking between bunches of them… the towering Columns of Thor, as they say. Thunderstorms can be good fun too but also very dangerous if you get caught inside one." Dom spotted a gap between two fluffy-looking innocent specimens and took *War-Weary* through the gap, which was beautifully illuminated by the rays of the afternoon sun.

"Dom, they are more beautiful than I could ever imagine."

"You're absolutely right but strange thing, you know, after you have been flying for a while, you just become blind to all the beauty. Some of the colours when the sun is coming up or going down, for instance, are absolutely fantastic." Silence reigned for a minute then Dom was back again.

"I guess you would like to see home and the water tower where all this started."

"Oh please, that would be terrific but… the time, it is going far too quickly."

"I'll give you a guided tour and then we'll take a look at Lintock on the way home. OK then, everyone knows that this part of England is chock-full of US airbases."

"Yes, why is that?"

"Closer to Europe for the bombers, I guess, and you guys have got Lincolnshire covered."

"Makes sense!"

Dom turned the old Mustang south-west, taking care to stay clear of various sensitive areas. Just because little was happening at Linton Grange today, it didn't mean some of the other stations weren't active.

"Dom, how do you find your way around up here?"

Dom chuckled. "Lots of practice and getting to know all the local landmarks, like towns, villages, railways, rivers and roads, even exceptional standout ones like your water tower. Most pilots will know the coastline from the Wash to the Thames Estuary like the back of their hand. It's kind of important when you are trying to find your way home."

"I can get that, so what is that airfield I can see ahead of us and slightly to the left?"

"That's Duxford. We call it the Duck Pond, home of the 78th." Dom gently put the Mustang into a slow turn. "Over to the left, that's Cambridge, and beyond it in the distance is station 374 Bottisham, where the 361st live, and over to the right, that's Little Walden… By the way, I hope you are not writing all this down because if you are, I may be forced to shoot you." Rose was laughing again.

"Behave, Captain, remember you are a visitor to my country." Dom's face was creased in a smile but he was still concentrating on the job in hand, and after scanning the airspace ahead, he smoothly rolled the aeroplane level and made some small adjustments to the trim so it would fly hands-off straight and level.

"Rose... would you like to have a go at controlling this old lady?"

"You're joking, I wouldn't know where to start."

"OK... Now gently place your hands on the control column and your feet on the pedals, gently now – I am going to ask you to make a turn to the right. To do that, you're going to push gently on the right pedal, it's the opposite to a bike, and move the stick a few degrees over to the right. When I tell you to bring the stick back to the middle and release the rudder pedals, she will stay where she is and continue to turn... Are you ready now? Move smoothly, as if you were immersed in oil." Rose was never good at doing what she was told, but this time she followed his instructions as if her life depended on it.

"I did it, I did it. I'm flying an aeroplane." Just to prove the point, Dom put both his hands behind his head for a few seconds.

"OK, Rose, I will take her back now."

"Not sure if I will let you, I'm getting such a buzz out of this. Nobody will ever believe me."

"Well, that's good because you are telling no one. If my boss finds out, I'm toast."

"So I have a hold over you."

"I'm finding out things about you today, Rose Collins…
and they're not all good."

"I'm a bad girl. I already knew that." Dom laughed out
loud; he had never known a girl like this before.

"Well, let's see if we can find Lintock and the water tower."
Within minutes, the Mustang was lined up with the redbrick
tower, which Rose had easily spotted.

"That's unfortunate."

Dom was concerned. "What's unfortunate, Rose?"

"I can't see any young women for you to terrorise."

"I'll get even with you later… how about giving your
house a fly-by? How do we find it?"

"Easy, just find the church and follow the river."

Dom took the Mustang down to 500 feet and did just that.
Rose was fascinated and gave Dom a running commentary
of everything she could see. He glanced at the fuel gauge and
turned the aeroplane for Linton Grange. "Well, I guess we
should start making tracks for home."

"Dom, something has occurred to me… see all those
fields of golden wheat and barley down there, well, the
harvest will be underway very soon and everybody will be
helping out, especially in the evenings. It would be a great
chance for you to get to know the villagers and make a good
impression on my dad."

Rose was regretting those last few words and was waiting
for him to say, *Why would I want to do that?* But no, he
was all for it. "Love to, but remember, I'm a city boy from
Belmont, New York. I wouldn't know one end of a pitchfork
from another."

"Well, you showed me how to fly an aeroplane, so I can
show you how to use a pitchfork."

"Rose… I don't know what evenings I will be free but… it's a deal… I promise." She leaned her head hard back against the headrest and closed her eyes; life didn't get much better than this!

Within minutes, they were back on the ground at Linton Grange and taxiing back towards the T2 hangar. Dom swung the Mustang round in a hard turn and had it parked only inches from where they had set out. The mechanic had left the chocks and canopy cover in a neat pile on the grass next to the parked Jeep, so putting old *War-Weary* to bed was easy.

The way off the base was just the reverse of coming on and once again the plan worked perfectly, with the duty policeman waving them through. A mile down the road, Dom pulled off the road and helped her out of her flight overalls, during which he accidently brushed her right breast. Before he could figure out what to say or do next, they were in a hard embrace and things were getting a little out of hand. He was just about to say, *Is this right?* when he was cut short by the noisy approach of bicycles, fifty or more of them one after another.

"Those bloody bicycles. Why do they have to pick my road?" Rose was convulsed with laughter.

"Rose… I think we should be getting you back. We don't want you to miss evening service, do we?"

Rose laughed and flopped back in the Jeep seat. "You are right, of course, but how can I thank you for this afternoon? It's been like nothing I could ever have imagined."

Dom wanted to say that he could think of something, but he had too much respect for her and simply softly replied, "Let's go then."

Yet another mission had been scrubbed for bad weather over Northern Germany. Finally, after five delays and sitting in their cockpits for what seemed like hours and hours in the summer heat, the squadron pilots were stood down for the day. They all clambered aboard the waiting Jeeps, which took them back to the squadron buildings. Gilburtson was in fine form. "SNAFU as usual, Command couldn't organise a beer party in a brewery – what can you do with half a day? It's too late to do anything. Of course... some luckier guys amongst us... have gorgeous young ladies they can visit." Gilburtson, Zetterval and Pepperman were looking at Dom.

"What... why are you guys looking at me like that? If you made a little more effort and tried to get to know the locality instead of rushing off to London at every opportunity, maybe your luck would change."

Gilburtson could not resist a response. "Yes, Captain, I'm sure we will keep that in mind in future... Tell you what, though, has the good captain thought about his choice of second career when this lot is all over? They sure as hell won't need all these pilots. I was thinking maybe of the priesthood, for myself, that is, of course."

Dom laughed; it was the only thing he could do. Vic Gilburtson had the knack of just staying this side of showing disrespect for rank and he knew he meant him no harm, and anyway he was a good fighter pilot and had saved Dom's bacon a few times when flying as his wingman, driving enemy fighters off his tail. "Actually, I'm going to help out in the local community this evening, so I know exactly what I'm doing."

"Oh yea, and where's that?"

"Like I would tell you."

"Got me there, Cap!" They were at the equipment centre, where they dumped their flight gear and made their way back to the huts.

*

Dom was getting to know the road to Lintock quite well now, and getting a Jeep was no problem. Funny how the promise of a quick flip in old *War-Weary* could oil the right wheels. It was a Wednesday and Rose had told him that by midweek they would be harvesting the upper fields near the water tower. Sure enough, as he crested the shallow rise, there was what looked like half the village busily stacking the sheaves of wheat into conical stooks, which would keep the grain heads off the ground prior to being collected for threshing. A horse-drawn binder was slowly circling the square of golden wheat, around which were positioned young boys armed with 'rabbit' sticks they had cut out of the roadside hazel hedges. Dom, who had borrowed a pair of old work fatigues, parked the Jeep on the narrow verge and vaulted the five-bar gate. A youth with a stick that appeared far too big for him bounded across to meet him. "Are you the man who has come to fix the binder, 'cause you're too late? Old Mr Cribb has fashioned a new pintle and, as you can see, she is working a treat."

"Well, actually, I'm here to lend a hand. Maybe you can help."

"Are you an American?"

"Sure am, buster… Oh, I see… Gum, is it?" Dom reached into his pocket and pulled out a packet of gum. "There you go… Now, sir, would you know if the Collins family are here, have you seen them?"

"Only Miss Rose, she is down in the corner near the big elm tree."

"Thanks, my man, let's hope you have good hunting. See you later." The boy turned and was off; it would be just his luck to get caught talking to a stranger when a monstrous great hare or rabbit came his way. Dom set off towards the elm tree, acknowledging workers as he passed them. There she was, no shrinking violet was Rose, tossing some of the drier sheaves up onto a cart. She was dressed in a pair of light brown dungarees over a white cotton blouse, with her hair tied back under a red and white gingham headscarf. She spotted him from 50 yards away.

"Dom, you made it."

"Well, I did promise." Dom explained the problems with the weather and how they had been stood down for the day. "Well, it could be raining here in an hour. That's why everyone is rushing about." She pointed across to the east, where ominous-looking summer thunder clouds were gathering. The cart was parked in the corner of the field and there was a convenient blind spot between it and the hedge. "Come with me and I will find you a fork."

Dom followed and once they were out of sight, they came together in an embrace. "God, I do miss you, Rose…"

She had her finger on his lips. "Shush… don't waste time talking. Just show me how much!"

Voices could be heard coming closer to the cart. "I suppose we should look like we are working." Rose handed him the spare pitchfork and they innocently made their way back to the front of the cart and continued the loading. It was two of the village ladies who were doing a round of the field with two giant earthenware flagons of cider, bringing well-earned refreshment to the harvest workers.

"I don't know if I qualify, ladies. I've only been here a short while."

"No matter, go ahead, we might not be around again before it starts raining." Dom stood there waiting for a glass to be proffered, but the ladies just handed him the jar.

Rose stepped in. "Drink it the country way, Dom, like this." She took a pace forward, rotated the jar onto the back of her right wrist, wiped the top with her other hand and took a slug.

Dom laughed. "Well, if that's the way it's done, here goes." Dom thanked them and the ladies started to move off towards the next group of workers, but not before giving Rose a wink of approval.

Dom rolled up his sleeves a little more and set to work. "You know, Rose, I could get a real liking for that stuff."

"Well, you wouldn't be the first, and probably not the last, but let's get this loaded before it starts raining."

Dom and Rose set to the task, and the wagon was loaded just before the first drops of warm summer rain started to fall. A breathless youth rushed up. "Farmer Smithy says we will call it a day and finish up tomorrow. Anybody who needs a lift is welcome to get a lift on the tractor and trailer, which will be going back to the farm by way of the village." Rose thanked him and sent him on his way and to tell Farmer Smith not to wait for them, as they had their own transport. By the time they had the tarpaulin on the wagon it was raining hard, forcing them to make a run for the Jeep.

Dom had the Jeep started but one of the top bow thumbscrews was jammed and he couldn't get the top up.

"Rose, you're soaked."

"Dom, don't worry about the top, just drive down this road. There is a track on the left and if you go up it a little way there is an old hay barn where we can shelter."

The rain was hammering down on the corrugated tin roof. Once through the door, they just stood there in the empty space. The noise was immense; it was like being inside a drum.

For a while, neither of them moved, both wondering what to do next, but then Rose's face took on a broad smile. "I know," she said as she pulled off her headscarf and shook her long auburn hair free, "catch me if you can." So saying, she sprinted for the ladder, which led up to the hayloft. This caught Dom completely by surprise but, laughing, he ran after her, but she was quick and was almost at the top of the ladder before he caught her by the ankle. He released his hold and they both fell into the soft, warm hay, panting with laughter.

"Rosie Collins," he said as they both rolled onto their backs, "if I did not know you better, I would think you were trying to lead me astray. What if the farmer appears looking for some hay?"

Rose laughed. "Well, it wouldn't be the first time I've gotten into trouble up here." Dom's face fell in disappointment. She laughed again but made a mocking scowl. "I didn't mean what you're thinking."

"What was I thinking?" Rose just laughed and carried on reminiscing as the rain started to ease. "I used to come up here with my brothers during the summer holidays. Mum would fix us up with a picnic and we would be gone all day, out on our bikes." Dom was listening intently. "We would make dens in all sorts of places, but this was always our favourite. We would pretend we were in the crow's nest of a pirate ship or stranded on some desert island. Oh, how I long for those carefree summer days before this wretched war."

"But you wouldn't have met me."

"That's true, but one day we were up here when Tommy, that's the younger of my two brothers, was trying to tightrope walk across that beam over there. He fell through the gap breaking his arm... Dad banned us from ever coming up here again."

"So that was the last time you were up here?"

Rose nodded. "But I still remember the sweet smell of the hay and the sun's rays peeping through the holes in the old corrugated tin roof... It hasn't changed a bit, still feels just as warm and comforting."

Dom's face relaxed and for a moment his mind drifted back home to the time when his summer vacation was shared with his brothers and friends on the streets of Belmont, but their upbringing was very different. She was a pure breath of country innocence, whilst he had developed an edge which had been hardened by the streets of New York.

Rose suddenly sat up and slipped the straps of her dungarees off her shoulders, pulling her blouse free. "My clothes are a bit wet, I just need to dry off a little," she said, flapping the white cotton edges.

Dom sat up beside her, taking in the glory of her soft damp auburn curls which fell around her pale English complexion, but today there was something a little different. What was it? "Just love those freckles on your nose and cheeks."

"What freckles? I haven't had freckles for years."

Dom chose to ignore that. "Rose, what would you say if I told you that you are the most beautiful girl I've ever known?"

"Guess you haven't known many then but go on."

Dom laughed. "And boy oh boy, I didn't know harvest time could be so much fun."

Rose replied by pulling him closer to her and kissing him fully on the mouth whilst whispering softly, "Neither did I."

Dom kissed her back, his tongue softly teasing her lips apart. Rose shuddered and pushed her breasts hard against him. His arms were around her now and he gently ran his hand down her back and under her blouse. His hand traced the curve of her waist round to her stomach and then slowly up to her breast, which he tenderly caressed. Rose had never felt like this before; she was in a different world. Yes, she had had the odd boyfriend or two from the village, one of whom she had kissed, but it was nothing like this. This felt so different here with Dom, and somehow she knew this was where life was leading her and so, standing up and feeling neither shame nor embarrassment, she undid the fastenings of her dungarees, which fell to the floor, and deftly stepped out of them. Dom reached up and, holding her hand, gently pulled her down into the hay. "Are you sure?" he said.

Rose just smiled, but looking into her big blue eyes, Dom knew that words were no longer necessary and they came together. With his first thrust, Rose caught her breath and let out a little cry. Dom paused but she pulled him closer, and there in the hay, with the sweet smell of summer, to the rhythm of the falling rain, Dom made love to his beautiful English Rose and she, to her captain... and Rose knew that this memory would stay with her until the day she died. Dom kissed her softly and stroked the hair gently away from her eyes. For his part, he knew that from this moment on, he would love and protect this girl forever.

EIGHT

JOURNEY'S END

Dom awoke the next day after a fitful sleep. He had been turning the pleasant memories of last night's events over and over in his mind, but along with those memories had arrived some questions that needed urgent answering. The morning had produced clarity. His life had taken an unexpected turning all right, but no doubts remained; he knew exactly what he should do.

Looking around at his roommates, he realised that he was the only one awake; typical, he thought, of fighter pilots to take advantage of a day with no mission planned to get an extra few minutes in the sack. Something else was still bothering him, though. A week ago, he had applied for a twenty-five-hour extension to his tour, but he had heard nothing. This was strange. Normally, such applications from experienced pilots were passed with little or no holdup. Could it be they had other plans for him?

He washed and dressed and strolled to breakfast at the mess, which contained the normal number of early risers, but something was different; there was an expectant buzz in the air. Curious as to what it was, he asked an acquaintance from another squadron, "What's up, why all the excited chatter?"

The reply sat him back on his heels. "Oh, some visiting pilots have started something."

"Oh yea, what's that?"

"Appears there is a strong rumour that one of the fighter groups up in Norfolk is getting ready to move over to France in support of the invasion."

"What, just a detached flight?"

"No, lock, stock and barrel apparently."

"You know what that means."

"Sure thing, we could all be heading that way."

Dom headed back to the hut, where he was greeted by Dave Zetterval, who was the only one up and dressed. "What's the news on the street, Captain?"

"Strong rumour going round in the mess!"

"Good one, I hope." Dom gave Zetterval the news, stressing it was just what he said, a rumour, nothing else, and not to plan on anything until it was official.

"France, eh? Just think of all those mademoiselles." Zetterval paused and then apologised; he had an important message for Dom.

"Sorry, Cap, I should have told you this straight away. You're needed at the group commander's office at 9:30. A messenger was just in here." Dom took a deep breath. What now? Probably some plan for a training exercise or an invitation to watch some military movie informing them how things should be done, made by people 3,000 miles away who were totally out of touch with reality. Looking at his wristwatch, he only had ten minutes. He grabbed his jacket and garrison side cap and then, muttering that his bicycle had better be there, disappeared down the corridor.

Dom walked into the large room outside the CO's office, where he found the group squadron commanders and other flight leaders all gathered around a large table. Nobody, it appeared, knew what was going on. The office door opened and with a cry of, "Att-hut," the room came to attention and Col John B. Danders entered the room, accompanied by a mystery major, whom, it appeared, nobody had ever seen before.

"Gentlemen, thank you for coming, but before we come to the main business of the day, I would like to introduce you to Major James Hadley... As most of you will probably know, he is the son of Senator George Hadley. The Major has served with distinction in the Far-East theatre, having completed a full tour there, and is now serving at Fighter Command Headquarters European Theatre. You will also know that our Group Executive Lt Col Bridge is on thirty days' well-earned rest leave in the US. During his absence, the Major here will be acting up as Group Executive Officer, so, I would like you all to welcome him." This came as somewhat of a shock to the assembled pilots, who had fully expected one of their own to be temporarily promoted, as was normal in these circumstances. The news, such as it was, was received with somewhat of an embarrassed muted silence. It was also apparent by the tone of his voice that the colonel was not too happy about the situation either. "But onto the main event, and I have to admit that the next couple of days are going to see a big change in the way we operate." Dom's mind was racing. *Here we go, a move across the Channel...* but no!

Turning to the sergeant at the door, the colonel barked, "Sergeant, bring the large map and lay it out on the table." The map was duly laid out on the table and weighted down at the corners. "There will be a secondary briefing this afternoon and a full briefing for everyone taking part tomorrow morning. However, gentlemen, basically, this is where we are at, with the situation in northern France."

The map showed an enlarged picture of the front line as it existed that day, showing the area around the northern French towns of Falaise and Argentan. The red line showed a deep inlet in the allied front line, forming what looked like a horizontal pocket or bag with a narrow opening to the east. "Gentlemen, two things can happen here. If the Germans break out to the west, a deep dividing line will be driven between the British and Canadians, along with the Polish 1st Armoured Division in the north and the two US Corps in the south. However, if we can pull the noose closed on the eastern neck of the pocket, tens of thousands of German troops and their equipment will be isolated and cut off. The Canadian and the Polish 1st armoured division are waiting to the north of the pocket neck on the high ground here." He pointed to a red mark on the map. "Waiting to strike and seal the German 7th Army off... but here is the deadly fly in the ointment. On the south side of the pocket neck, sheltering in front of this high ground here," once more, he pointed to the map, "the Germans have arranged lines and lines of mobile 88mm guns and Tiger tanks, and any attempt to seal off the pocket by the Canadians and Poles must surely result in them being blasted off the map and their total destruction."

One of the squadron commanders said what everyone was thinking. "Can't see where we can help, sir. Our speciality is long-range bomber escort, and surely this is a job for the tactical department or the heavies."

"Oh, they have tried but they can't get the accuracy. In the case of the heavies, we end up hitting our own troops and the tactical B-26s. Well, they are restricted by this high ground behind the guns. They just can't get low enough." The colonel continued. "The P-51 is an excellent high-and mid-altitude escort fighter, but we all know that at very low altitude, she is extremely vulnerable to ground fire. A single riffle bullet through the coolant system has brought many a Mustang down. No, the aeroplanes for this are the rocket- and bomb-carrying P-47 Thunderbolts of the 9th, which have already carried out quite a few of these sort of missions."

The same squadron commander who had raised the first question was quick to interject. "Sorry to interrupt, sir, but I still can't see where we fit into the plan."

"Well, the Germans aren't stupid. They know that whatever the outcome is, whether it be their withdrawal to the east or an outbreak thrust to the west, this gap to the east of Falaise must, for them, stay open. They are well aware that we have been trying, unsuccessfully, to soften up the 88s and Tigers to give the Canadians and Poles a chance, so they are keeping massed standing Fw190 patrols over the area. To be blunt, the P-47 is built like a brick outhouse and can take a huge amount of punishment, but we also know that its low-level climb performance is poor. If they are caught by the Fw190s during their approach or slow climb out over this high ground, they could be decimated... Gentlemen, it will be your job to stop that happening."

Someone remarked that didn't the 9th have their own P-51s, to which Danders replied, "Yes," but not enough.

Someone else quipped that he never thought they would end up wet nursing Thunderbolts. This received a few laughs but, in general, the mood was sombre. The colonel had a few extra points to make in that there would be a pre-mission briefing for all squadron commanders and flight leaders at 14:00 and that all rostered pilots for tomorrow would be confined to camp for the evening in order that everyone got a good night's sleep. They had heard this story before. What he really meant was that nobody would have the opportunity to get involved with what the Limeys referred to as 'Careless talk cost lives'. The colonel did have one important further point to finish off with, however: "This mission, gentlemen, is going to be one of the most critical you have ever taken part in. However, I have one deep regret... Command have insisted that as I have led the last three consecutive missions, I should stand down for this one... Major Hadley as the acting air executive will lead. As I have said, he has a vast amount of experience and I have one hundred per cent confidence that he will do an excellent job, Thank you, gentlemen."

Dom went back to his quarters and gave his three pilots what news he could about the upcoming mission. Gilburtson asked the obvious question. "What's so special about this mission that it requires two briefings and special security? Why can my crew chief and his assistant go down to the Pear Tree in the village and have a pint tonight, but we can't? It makes no sense."

"Sorry, Vic, I can see your frustration, but you'll find out all the details at tomorrow morning's briefing. If you need a beer, you can always get one at the OC." Gilburtson shrugged his shoulders and sat down on his bed.

*

The secondary briefing went without a hitch and Dom had to admit that he was quite impressed with the new acting air executive's planning. As they left this morning's meeting, there had been some mumblings about West Point graduates and the pulling of strings by certain politicians for the military advancement of their relatives, but the mood had now changed. The senior pilots were now much happier. Hadley had kept it simple, giving the route to the target and the map reference squares they would occupy, effectively sealing off the Fw190 standing patrols from the P-47s. He also stressed that flight leaders should ensure that they briefed their pilots on the careful management of fuel and the use of the Mustang's wing, body and drop tanks. This mission, although much shorter than usual, could call for combat at any time, and pilots should not be caught out by centre of gravity control issues caused by poor fuel management.

The full mission briefing, even earlier than normal next morning, not unexpectedly, caused quite a reaction. This was something very different and the pilots were on edge but once again, Major Hadley answered all questions and explained in detail exactly what was required. His briefing was followed by an address by the group CO, Colonel Danders. "Gentlemen... I cannot emphasise how important the mission you will fly today is, both in terms of the protection you will be providing for the P-47s – and believe me, their task is difficult, they will be flying in at an angle of 30 degrees and letting their rockets go only 400 yards from the target – and, of course, this maybe even more important, what a successful outcome will mean to our US boys and their allies on the ground." The briefing continued in the normal way and at its end the pilots headed out, making their way to the squadron ready room buildings, a procedure they had followed so many times before.

Dom briefed Red Flight; today, they would be part of two flights, which made up one section of the two-section squadron, making sixteen fighters in all. Major Tom Backersly would lead the two flights of the lower lead section with Dom leading the other two flights of the high section. Their squadron call sign was BEARBACK. The other two squadrons would be CHURCHYARD and REDSKINS, making up between the three squadrons forty-eight P-51s in total. All squadrons would communicate on radio Channel 'A', and Major Hadley would lead the mission from REDSKINS White flight with the code name CROCODILE Leader.

The flight to the target area was conducted in good weather and although uneventful it was very different in that the journey down to France was very much on a southerly heading. They were far more used to climbing hard and heading due east. Secondly, they crossed the coast at only 15,000 feet, much lower than normal. This was possible because the entry point was over Normandy, which was, or should have been, friendly territory. Even so, several black umbrella-shaped bursts of flak appeared, some of which were far too close for comfort. The P-47s, which had refuelled on the English south coast, were flying 2,000 feet below them and trailing by about 5 miles. The plan was for the P-51s to mix it with the Fw190s, leaving the P-47s a free run to the 88s and Tigers.

The P-51s skirted along the northern edge of the pocket, all eyes peeled for the patrolling Fw190s. They passed the town of Falaise to the south and still nothing. The P-47s were holding off to the western edge of the pocket where they would form up and attack in pairs every thirty seconds by sliding along the southern edge of the pocket and then cutting into the west of Chambois.

Major Hadley was on the radio. "Crocodile Leader here, anyone see the 190 patrols?" There was no reply; something was not quite right. They had crossed the front line and were now well over German-held territory. There were no German fighters but some light flak. This was too good to be true. Hadley was on the radio again. "Crocodile Leader here, hold formation and carry out the racetrack pattern patrol as planned."

There was a shout from one of the pilots. "There they are, way over to the east, looks like fifty plus." All pilots craned their necks, searching for the threat. But the enemy fighters appeared hesitant to engage and continued to circle at a distance well out of range. The P-51 pilots readied themselves for action. Dom, who had been turning other things over and over in his mind, was now fully focused, as it looked like they would have to take the fight to the enemy.

Yet again, Hadley was on the radio. "Crocodile Leader here, we will stay where we are and keep this area protected."

The first pair of P-47s started their attack. The rockets, which were crude to say the least, were launched through long tubes which were no more than modified versions of the type used by the infantry. The first two salvos missed by a country mile, but the others would learn from their experience. The P-51s pilots on the west side of the formation had a grandstand view of the attack, but then there was a yell from a member of CHURCHYARD Squadron. "Christ, look behind the next pair of Jugs, 109s. Where in hell did they come from?"

Both P-47s were now going down in flames; they didn't stand a chance. Dom, like the rest of the pilots, was assessing the situation, got it. The Fw190s were just a decoy. Those 109s had been hiding low to the south of Argentan and for them it was like shooting fish in a barrel. Hadley had to make a decision and make it quick. "Crocodile Leader here, we stay where we are and keep the Fw190s away from the Bolts."

There was silence and anger; this wasn't the way this group did things. Another P-47 smashed into the ground in a rolling fireball. Three in less than a minute; they were getting decimated. Dom reacted in the only way he knew how: he keyed his radio. "Bearback Red Leader here, I have radio failure, I can transmit only. Assume the order to attack those 109s has been given." He rolled the *Guardian Angel* onto her port wingtip, put her nose down and headed for the black mass of Me109s, who were queuing up to knock down the Thunderbolts.

Pepperman, Gilburtson and Zetterval followed without hesitation or question, and very soon, so did Blue Flight, quickly followed by Tom Backersly and the whole of the lead low section. Hadley was frozen; he didn't know what to do! Surely, they must stick to the plan and keep a barrier in place between the Fw 190s and the P-47s. His jumbled thought process was jarred back into action by another radio call. "Churchyard Leader here, I have radio failure, following Bearback down." All sixteen aeroplanes of Churchyard Squadron plunged after their comrades, leaving only the sixteen Redskins aeroplanes in place; thirty-two versus fifty plus... that was much fairer odds.

Well, the die had now been well and truly cast; they were all in this together. Low-level air combat was not their forte, but they would give as good as they got. Dom led Red Flight head-on, straight into the mass of 109s, who were breaking left, right and centre as they screamed through the packed formation. Once out the other side, he gave the order, every man for himself. The sky was full of twisting, turning Me109s and P-51s. A Me109 came at Dom head-on and they made several passes, both firing at each other. On the third pass, he got some strikes on the German's engine and a large engine cowling panel fell away. Seconds later, it rolled over and went down in a lazy spiral before crashing in some woods. Dom looked in his mirror and craned his neck round left and right. No Pepperman, no anybody, but they were big boys now. They could look after themselves.

His second victory was more difficult. He noticed a P-47 in a turning fight with a 109. They were in a Luftbury, each trying to turn inside the other. The P-47 appeared to be gaining on the 109 but as it started firing, the 109 tightened his turn. The P-47 tried to follow but mushed to the outside, losing his advantage. Dom came in from underneath and gave a long burst, registering several hits on the Messerschmitt's wings and body. A huge cloud of coolant exploded in front of the cockpit, and the 109 gently dipped its nose and crashed into a yellow cornfield. Dom's ammunition was now running low. Maybe it was time to make an exit. Over to the north, the last of the P-47s, now unmolested, were launching their rockets. He looked to the east but he could see nothing of Redskin Squadron, but right now he didn't care. He had disobeyed an order. If this was the end, so be it. He had done like his father had always told him: *When in doubt, do the right thing.* He headed north for home.

No point in hanging about; the attack was over. He could see the coast of Normandy ahead but also two specks heading the same way as him but travelling much slower; must be part of the group going home like him, but no, there were flashes coming from the wings of the second aircraft. It was an Fw190 trying to finish off a crippled Mustang. He shoved the throttle through the gate and made chase. At extreme maximum range, he opened fire, more in hope and desperation than anything else. The pilot of the Fw190 took evasive action and turned away to the east. On catching up with the Mustang, Dom realised to his horror that it was his wingman, Pepperman. "Are you OK, Red Two?"

The reply came back. "Not really, my left leg is smashed. I'm bleeding like a stuck pig and, what's more, my port aileron is jammed."

"OK now, first things first, can you tie anything round your leg to slow down the bleeding?"

"I've done that, used my oxygen hose. Kind of figured I wouldn't need it anymore today."

"That's fine. We're over the coast now, just the Channel to cross. We will get you down in one of the emergency fields on the south coast."

They were now nearly halfway across the Channel when Dom's world was torn asunder by the sound of 20mm cannon. It was the same Fw190. "Jesus, don't you ever give up?" He swung the *Angel* round in a sharp arc and just before the 190 was about to finish Pepperman off, he pulled the gun trigger. There was a short burst and then it stopped. He was out of ammunition, but that last burst was enough to make his adversary turn away. However, the 190 had not left the scene. It was keeping a close watch on them whilst just keeping out of range. Dom considered… was the bastard coming back for a third go? *Sure enough, here he comes again.* They were defenceless. Maybe he could bluff him, only he knew he was out of ammo, but then just as he was about to turn into him, the Fw190 veered away, heading due east. But why, why did he do that? And then he realised, because there, right in front of him, was the beautiful shape of two patrolling RAF Spitfire Mk 9s who had seen what was happening and were now tearing after the Fw190, who was making for the French coast as fast as it could.

Dom made an emergency radio call and was vectored in to RAF Westhampnett, where medical services would be available. He radioed Pepperman. "OK, Pep, stay with me. We are going to put you down at RAF Westhampnett. It's almost straight in front of us."

"OK, but you are going to have to buddy me in because my airspeed indicator is bust. In fact, most of my instruments are out."

"No problem, I will see you in, OK?"

The pair made a gentle turn and lined up with the runway. "OK, let's try a little flap and see if they work." Pepperman did exactly that and, miracle of miracles, they did.

"OK, good sign, this must be your lucky day."

To this, Pepperman replied in a low voice, "I don't think so."

"Good to see your sense of humour is still in place… all we need now is for the gear to come down and we will be home and dry but… wait, wait until I call it, OK?" The approach continued with Dom calling out the speed and asking for small incremental changes in power. The gear did come down and Pepperman, accompanied by Dom, who was flying just off his port wingtip, placed the damaged Mustang on the long runway with little or no fuss and rolled to a halt. At the last minute, just before Pepperman flared, Dom had powered the *Angel* away into an overshoot and a low left-hand circuit off of which he had landed. He taxied to where the other Mustang had come to a halt, pulled onto the hard grass and shut down. By the time he was out of the cockpit, the RAF emergency crew had already extracted Pepperman and were loading him into the back of a large green ambulance. Dom managed to get a glimpse of him before they shut the doors, but his wingman was unconscious. He ran over and managed to grab one of the medics. "Hey, bud, can you do me an important favour?"

"Will if I can, what is it?"

"Once he has been assessed, can you get a message to Doc Pearson at USAAF fighter station 391 Linton Grange? He will want the full lowdown on Lt Pepperman's condition and to be given any news."

"Certainly do my best, but we should be moving. He looks like he's lost a lot of blood."

Dom nodded and the ambulance pulled away towards the group of buildings on the far side of the airfield. He walked across to Pepperman's aircraft, jumped up on to the left wing root and glanced inside the cockpit. After getting over the initial shock of seeing so much blood, he could see what had happened. A 20mm shell had passed right through the fuselage, entering low on the left-hand side and exiting high on the right, just below the canopy rail. Mercifully, the round had not exploded. He was brought back to the moment by a crisp, very English accent; it was the RAF station duty officer. "I'm afraid we are going to have to clear the runway, sir."

Dom nodded. He glanced at his watch; it was still only 12:30.

"Do you need fuel, sir?"

"No, I should be OK – if you have someone standing by with a fire extinguisher whilst I start, I'll be away directly." This was quickly arranged and within ten minutes the *Guardian Angel* was airborne and heading back to Linton Grange.

Dom taxied past the line of parked Mustangs, noticing several gaps, including Pepperman's and his own. Oddly sitting at the far end of the line was a visitor, a B-26 Marauder, obviously being worked on. Dick Ferra was there to greet him. "Sorry to hear about Lt Pepperman, sir."

"Well, it could be worse. At least he is in good hands... Dick, what's up with the B-26 Widow Maker on the end there?"

"Oh, you mean the *Baltimore Whore*."

"That's a bit strong. I understand the Baltimore bit, but why whore?"

"Very fast and no means of visible support, the short wing thing!"

"Oh, I see, and why is she here?"

"Lobbed in early this morning on a delivery flight from Burtonwood to Stansted, misfiring engine problem apparently. As Stansted was socked in with a summer thunderstorm, they decided to come in here. They have been working on the No 1 engine for a couple of hours now and oh... I have a message from the pilot... he says he knows you from your high school days and will catch up with you later."

"Who the hell could that be? Anyway, thanks, Dick. I ought

to get back to the squadron for a late debrief. Ah, here's my transport. Not much wrong with the *Angel*, by the way, never is."

He turned away towards the Jeep with Dick Ferra calling after him, "No radio problems, Dom, sir?"

Dom chuckled. "What do you think?"

The Jeep made its way back to the group interrogation room with Dom thinking about the morning and how it had all panned out. The realisation was now dawning on him that there would be plenty of questions about his actions over Falaise to be answered.

Dom entered the interrogation room. It was nearly empty; the intelligence officer was seated at his desk and waved him across. "Captain D'Angelino, take a seat or maybe you'd like to collect a coffee and doughnut before we talk."

Dom turned and saw the Red Cross girl, who was smiling at him. "Sure, if that's OK." Dom told the whole story and was amazed when the intelligence officer made no comment on his radio failure. Dom was puzzled; something was going on but he could not figure it out. His two victories would be confirmed if the gun camera had validated it.

"That will be all, Captain, and by the way, the colonel wants everybody who flew the mission today to report to the briefing room at 2:30."

Just as he was about to leave, Doc Pearson came in. "Thought I would find you here, Dom. I have just had a phone call from the hospital where they have taken Lt Pepperman."

"What's the news, Doc, good or bad?"

"Bit of both. The good news is he will live. The not-so-good news is that it will be a while before he walks again, and the likelihood of him ever flying again is very slim."

"Well… that's something, Doc. Probably get a Purple Heart and fly him home." That sounded cynical and he regretted it, but he did not have to apologise. Doc Pearson knew the signs of battle fatigue and Dom was near the edge. "Get yourself to the post-mission meeting and then have a good rest. I'm taking you off flying for three days."

Dom wasn't arguing with that, and anyway, he had a good idea what the outcome of the briefing would be… and it wasn't good.

"Anyway, thanks, Doc. Thanks for everything." He turned and made his way back to the officers' accommodation huts where he was warmly greeted by Gilburtson, Zetterval and a stranger who was sitting on the edge of Pepperman's empty bed.

"Marco Maggio, I wondered who it could be. How long has it been now and how did you know I was here?"

Maggio shook his hand. "You were a year in front of me at high school so probably four years or more… As for how I knew you were here, well, I found that out in a recent letter from my mother."

"Your mother!"

"Sure, apparently, you were front-page news in the *Belmont Globe* a couple of weeks back, big article and picture about *Local Boy Makes Ace Fighter Pilot*. By the way, where is the dog in the picture?" Dom laughed and explained about the borrowed Bentley.

"We must catch up but right now, these guys," he turned to Gilburtson and Zetterval, "probably want an update on Pep. Plus, we all have to attend a post-mission meeting in twenty minutes, which, to say the least, will probably be quite lively."

"No problem, I'll be in the OC with a cup of coffee."

As the three pilots made their way to the briefing room, Dom explained the story and situation with Pepperman. The two lieutenants handled the news in a philosophical manner. It had to be that way; this was not the first time they had lost a colleague through injury or death, and it would not be the last.

Dom, Gilburtson and Zetterval entered the briefing room and sat in the first row of seats, as there was no way they were going to hide from their actions earlier that day. They wanted to be seen and to be heard. The room quickly filled and bang on 2:30 they were called to attention with the arrival of Col John B. Danders, who marched briskly to the stage. Strangely, he was unaccompanied... so where was Major Hadley?

Danders addressed his audience. "As you may all know, I have served in the ETO from the very beginning, starting way back in May '42 and... I have to say that in the intervening years between then and now, I have never ever been associated with what I can only describe as the debacle of a performance which happened this morning over France. For thirty-two of my pilots to wilfully disobey a direct order from the mission leader and to take things into their own hands as you certainly did, is just way past comprehension in any shape or form. How certain experienced and senior pilots, and I'm looking at you, Captain D'Angelino and Major Backersly, took the action you did using one of the oldest bullshit excuses in the book, radio failure, my ar—"

At this point, the colonel, who was obviously very angry, was interrupted by a shout from his audience. "You would have done the same thing, Colonel."

He glared at the group of pilots in front of him then composed himself. "Silence, there will be no more outbursts.

What you have to get into your thick skulls is what we're trying to run here is a fighter group not a damned three-ring circus." He paused again and then changed tack. "Initial reconnaissance reports that the strikes by the P-47 Thunderbolts were successful and the capability of the defending 88s and Tiger Tanks has been seriously depleted." There was a loud cheer from the floor. "And... I also have a message here from the CO of that Thunderbolt Group thanking the Mustangs of this group for their timely intervention, which undoubtedly saved them from far more serious damage than the three ships and pilots that they lost. Without your protection, they would have lost far, far more." There was another even louder cheer from the floor.

"By the way, the radio failures must have been down to a faulty batch of tubes. I will have the radio department look into it." This was followed by laughter. "I will not say well done, and you know the reason why, but let's just say, today was a proud day for this fighter group but... and I mean this, if it ever happens again, I will have every one of you arrested and locked up in the jug. Is that understood? Now if there are no more questions... you are dismissed."

Somebody asked what everyone was thinking. "Where is Major Hadley, sir?"

Danders picked his words carefully. "Major Hadley has gone back to HQ Fighter Command. We came to a mutual agreement that maybe he was better suited to his old job of planning rather than in Operations. Oh and I will be appointing a new acting exec tomorrow." So saying, he came down from the stage and left the room to a rousing chorus of appreciation.

Dom made his way over to the Officers' Club and, sure enough, there was Marco chatting to one of the Red Cross girls behind the counter. He sneaked up behind him and said to the girl, "Don't believe a word he says. He's an Italian, you know."

Marco turned and punched Dom softly in the shoulder. "Never sneak up on a Widow Maker pilot like that... You know we live on the edge of our nerves."

The waitress asked if she could make a couple of coffees for them, which they gratefully accepted. "Go sit over there. I'll bring them across." Dom was now completely relaxed; three days' rest and he would borrow the Jeep again tonight and see Rose.

As they sat at the table, it occurred to him that this was the very table where he had first met her on that night of the dance. Marco was talking about the problems with the B-26 and Dom was only half listening; he still had visions of that evening in the hayloft. But this was no good; he should pay attention to what was being said.

"Actually, the new model, with slighter bigger wings and more powerful engines, is a big improvement, and accidents have dropped dramatically. Having said that, she is still a bit of a handful on take-off or landing if you lose an engine. Which is why I diverted in here, when we had that engine problem."

Dom nodded. "So have they fixed it?"

"I hope so but this is a strange one because it's a brand-new aeroplane, straight out of Burtonwood. They have changed the plugs and got a new ignition harness from somewhere. My mechanic has given her a full power run and apparently the engine has checked out fine."

Dom nodded and added, "So it's nothing to do with the prop control problems they suffer from?"

"Oh, you mean the dreaded Curtiss electric pitch change mechanism that can be a real headache if one lets go... full prop runaway, and you know where that can end, but things have improved. Basically, the secret is regular maintenance and checks to make sure it's all set up properly." Marco went on to explain that he was delivering the aeroplane with a crew of just two – him and a mechanic – no need for a co-pilot or navigator for this short trip.

Dom started to steer the conversation away from aeroplanes. He'd had enough of them for one day; he felt they needed to talk about something lighter. "And what's life like in the 9th, much the same as here, I guess?"

Marco laughed. "No lack of excitement, mainly mid- and low-level stuff."

Dom nodded. "We just ran a low-level escort mission this morning, and let's just say it wasn't short on excitement either, but enough of that. Stansted, why, that's much closer to London than us, so I guess you spend a lot of free time down there."

Marco hesitated. "Well, quite a bit but, to be honest, those Piccadilly commandoes scare me half to death."

"Ah, your mother never told you about them."

Marco laughed. "Too damn right, she didn't. How about you, have you got a regular girl?"

"Sure have, a real find, we are getting quite serious."

"Well, good for you, my man."

At this point, their coffee arrived, after which the conversation drifted back and forth, covering everything from baseball to news of old friends and the girls they had known in their youth. Dom deliberately avoided mentioning his old long-term New York girl who had sent him the *Dear*

John letter. That part of his life was over. What he had now, pushed all of that into insignificance. As the hands of the club clock reached 16:00, Marco said his goodbyes. He had better be getting back to the aeroplane. With a bit of luck, they would be away by 18:30. Dom apologised. Unfortunately, he couldn't be there to see them off, as about then he should be well on his way to Lintock.

There was a problem with the Jeep. Someone else had beaten him to it, but if he just waited fifteen minutes, another one would become available. Eventually, now nearly thirty minutes late, he was on his way, motoring along the road that skirted the base's southern boundary. His keen ear picked up the sound of two Pratt & Whitney R-2800 Double Wasp radial engines being put through their paces on the end of the runway. It was Marco taking the B-26 back to Stansted. Slowing down, he steered the Jeep to a place where he could watch the take-off. Leaving the engine running, he stepped out to get a better view.

The Double Wasps roared and the B-26 surged along the runway and smoothly rotated into the air. Dom started to turn away but just as he did there was the unmistakeable sound of a badly misfiring engine, and he watched in horror as the aeroplane dropped out of view behind some trees. The good engine was giving all it could, but it wasn't enough. There was a viscous crumping noise then all sound stopped. The B-26 was down and, what's more, as it was well away from the base, it would be some time before the duty fire trucks got here.

He jumped in the Jeep and sped off in the general direction of where the Marauder had disappeared behind the trees. There it was, flat on its belly in the middle of a wheat field, apparently still in one piece but with wisps of smoke coming from the centre section. Dom's brain was working overtime; if the corn caught fire, they wouldn't stand a chance. He stopped the Jeep, vaulted the fence and tore across the field. As he approached the B26, he was desperately trying to remember where the escape hatches were located and then he remembered: on top, they opened up like clam shells. But how in hell did you get up there? All the time there was a loud sizzling sound coming from the starboard engine; no time to think about that. He grabbed hold of anything he could and hauled himself up level with the cockpit. It was empty and the escape hatch on the other side was up… they had got out on the other side! There was a rumble, then an all-encompassing roar as the fuel in the starboard wing main tank ignited and exploded… Captain Domenico D'Angelino's world froze, turned progressively orange and then a brilliant white before fading slowly back to black!

NINE

ENGLAND – 20TH JUNE 2005

The gunmetal grey BMW E30 3 Series convertible signalled right and moved to the centre of the road before smoothly turning in between the tall gate pillars of the entrance to Cherry Wood Hall. From the main Cambridge Road, a first glance might well deceive a casual observer into thinking that this was some large country estate or expensive private school. Well set back from the road with its imposing mock gothic frontage and wide green lawns, it looked the embodiment of rich living from a bygone age. But appearances can be deceptive; this was Cherry Wood Hall Mental Health Hospital.

The BMW, keeping well to the 10 MPH speed limit, purred along the wide drive between the rows of mature purple beech trees, passing on the left a single-storey modern building and its secure 12-foot chain link fence. At the end of the drive, 50 yards further on, it turned right under a wide stone arch into the visitors' car park, where it was parked easily in two neat movements. Kirsten Davies stepped from the car, locked it and made her way towards the main entrance door situated at the top of a short but wide set of stone steps. As she was approaching the entrance, she noticed that a photographer was busying himself making minor adjustments to his photographic equipment, obviously intent on taking an image of the Victorian frontage. Not wishing to ruin all his good work, Kirsten stopped and waited patiently. What was an extra minute or two? And anyway, she had done a lot of waiting recently. To her complete surprise, the photographer looked up and started walking briskly towards her. "Excuse me, miss, would you be so kind as to stand on the steps for a moment and look in this direction?" he said, pointing with his hand. "A little human interest can add great value to a picture."

"Will the image be put to any commercial use?" She had no idea why she had spoken those words; they sounded very precocious.

"Possibly, would that be a problem?"

"No, not really. I guess I'm just trying to satisfy my own curiosity."

"Let me explain but first let me introduce myself. I'm William Benjamin, recently retired. I'm writing a book on the history of the old hospital and, of course, there is not much time left now before they start moving out the last of the patients to the new block on the other side of the hospital estate.

Kirsten was shocked. "They are moving patients out!"

"I'm so sorry, I should have asked. For some reason, I had assumed you were staff, so you must be a visitor. I really do

141

apologise. I should have been far more discreet." He started to turn back towards his camera and tripod.

Kirsten was a little confused. "I'm here to visit my great-aunt in Apple Tree Ward. Do you still want me to stand on the step for the photograph?"

William Benjamin, looking slightly downcast, stopped in his tracks and turned again towards Kirsten. "Did you say Apple Tree Ward?"

"I did indeed, is that so unusual?"

"No, not really, but please wait there a moment." He rushed over to his camera bag and returned with a business card which he pressed into her hand. "Miss, if in the future you ever need help on any subject to do with the history of Cherry Wood Hall, please do not hesitate to call me on this number, and yes, if it's OK with you, I would very much like to take that photograph."

Kirsten, slightly confused about the conversation of the last minute or so, strolled to the top of the steps and put on her best airline captain boarding pose. William Benjamin took a couple of images, thanked her and waved her on.

She made her way to the main reception area feeling a little angry. How come she, as the main and probably only regular visitor of her ageing great-aunt, had not been informed of these pending changes?

Yes, her Aunt Kathryn was one of the patients who were due to be moved to the new purpose-built block. "Is there a reason why my family was not informed?" Kirsten had the bit firmly between her teeth, and the receptionist, after first apologising, checked on the system.

"I'm sorry to say, madam, that you were informed. A letter was sent to Mr James Davies three weeks ago." Kirsten was not mollified by this answer; all it did was transfer her anger from the hospital to her father and stepmother. The receptionist then enquired, "Are you here to visit your great-aunt?"

"I certainly am. Do not worry about accompanying me. I know the way very well."

"Certainly, Miss Davies, but do take care. It's a little empty in Apple Tree. Most of the few remaining patients have already been transferred."

"Thank you, I'm deeply sorry if I may have been a little short with you when I arrived, and if I can leave this contact telephone number with you, then hopefully any future misunderstanding can be avoided."

"No problem, Miss Davies. I hope your aunt enjoys your visit."

Kirsten made her way along the old linoleum-covered hallway, her heels clicking as she progressed. The ward occupation board had only one name on it: Room No1, Kathryn Alexander. The special notes column was blank. At Room No1, she knocked on the door and waited; a delicate voice answered immediately. "Come in." Kirsten entered and beheld her great-aunt sitting in an easy chair by the window, staring at the outdoors. The pleasure in her aunt's blue eyes was palpable. "Kirsten, my love, come on over and give your old aunt a hug. Where have you been? It seems months since you were last here, and what's happened to your hair?"

Kirsten held her aunt's frail, delicate body in her arms and gave her a long hug. "Well, Aunt Kathryn, I had a flying accident and I've had a long stay in hospital, but I'm fine now. As for my hair, well… this is a wig."

"Oh lovely, can I try it on?"

Kirsten laughed; that was so typical of her aunt. "Behave, Aunty, you are supposed to show me some pity."

"Pity is a word I find hard to swallow, but tell me all about what happened."

This was obviously one of Kathryn's better days, and nobody could predict which of her days would be good or bad. Sometimes, like today, she was completely lucid and anyone could hold a normal conversation with her. On others, she would appear to drift off into a parallel world full of imaginary characters and sometimes even venom. Today, she sat quietly listening, her countenance with those penetrating blue eyes and classic bone structure still showing evidence of the beauty of her youth. Kirsten quickly related the events of the last few months and then paused. "But, Aunty, enough of me. What would you like to do?"

"Can we walk in the garden?"

"I don't see why not. I'll just pop along to the duty nurse and check if it's OK. You just wait here, I'll only be a minute."

Kirsten was soon back with the good news. "It's fine, Aunty. Let's go and find that rose garden."

Her aunt hesitated for a moment and then replied, "Yes, dear." They strolled slowly along the paved walk, making for the walled garden where, against its south-facing external wall, long ago, the estate gardener of the time had constructed a small but beautiful rose garden. With a little luck, the memorial seat that had been located there would be unoccupied, and they could sit in peace amongst the splendid colours and scented luxury, with the vista of the Gog Magog Hills rolling away into the distance. "Aunty, I understand they are going to move you to a brand-new facility on the other side of the hospital. Promise me you won't be difficult."

"Oh, they have already tried. Of course I won't be difficult, I'll just refuse to go."

Kirsten laughed. "I hope you're joking." Aunt Kathryn didn't reply; she was staring at the distant small shapes of cars as they sped along the long straight Cambridge Road.

The time passed all too quickly, but it was not Kirsten who suggested they start to make their way back; it was Aunt Kathryn, who was clearly becoming agitated. "Looks like we are in for some rain. I can see a summer storm gathering over there. I hope they have finished getting the harvest in."

Kirsten looked to where her great-aunt was pointing, but there was nothing but clear blue sky. "Are you sure, Aunty?"

"Oh yes, I must be getting back and of course I have to think about my other visitor, if they have finished the harvest. Why, he could be here shortly." Kirsten's face fell; her aunt had obviously slipped back into her other world and it was useless to try and argue otherwise. She gently placed her hand under Aunt Kathryn's arm and helped her to her feet.

"Well, we had better get going then."

During the journey back to her parents' house in Hertford, Kirsten reflected on everything that had happened that day. Aunt Kathryn seemed little changed but Kirsten was concerned about what sort of impact this move would have on a frail old lady who was fast approaching her 80th birthday. She was well aware that moving long-term mental patients from one facility to another could be extremely traumatic for them. Why on earth had her parents not told her? At dinner that night, her father informed her that there was a recorded message for her on the answerphone. Her company had been trying to contact her, as apparently there was a slight problem with the results of her last medical tests that needed discussing.

"Fine, I'll call them tomorrow. By the way, was there a letter from the hospital about relocating Aunt Kathryn?"

"Not that I know of. Have you seen anything, dear?" He turned and looked at his wife.

"Now you mention it, there was something but I didn't open it. Anything to do with that crazy old woman always means trouble."

"That's so unkind. Apart from Dad, she is my only living blood relative. I think we owe her something." Kirsten had long been aware that as far as her stepmother was concerned, Aunt Kathryn was a taboo family subject, to be avoided at all costs. She was of the opinion that if, God forbid, it ever got out that they had a relative in a mental institution, why, it must surely scupper any further advancement her husband could make in the police force.

The evening dragged by with several periods of embarrassing silence. Kirsten was angry with her stepmother for being so mean and narrow-minded and her father for being so weak. She picked up the letter from the hospital, which had miraculously reappeared, took it up to her room and opened it, but it contained nothing she hadn't found out already. Her big regret was that if she had known about the move sooner, she may have been able to do something about it and soften the blow a little.

The atmosphere showed little improvement at breakfast, so over the toast and coffee, she let them know that maybe it was for the best if she moved back into her Cheshunt flat. She felt perfectly well now and it was time, she thought, that she should try and get her life back on track. Basically, she had been living out of a suitcase for far too long and needed some stability, so after lunch, she loaded up the BMW and said her goodbyes.

*

The next morning didn't bring normality; contact with her company brought more trouble, the eye specialist had concerns that the last series of tests had shown that although improving, the level of vision in her left eye was still marginally below that required for the reissue of her CPL (Commercial Pilot Licence). He was convinced that given another month, her recovery would be complete, but meanwhile he could not recommend that she return to work. Apparently, she could still drive but… it was another four weeks of waiting and although it was difficult to explain, she had a strange feeling of foreboding.

*

Two days later at eight o'clock in the morning, she received a phone call which brought her feelings sharply and tragically into an explained focus. It was from the Cherry Wood Hall Hospital.

"Miss Davies, I'm afraid I have some very sad news for you… Your Great-Aunt Kathryn has sadly passed away."

Kirsten was shocked. "But I only saw her a few days ago. She was as well as I've seen her in a long time."

"I'm afraid it often happens this way. Today, as you know, she was due to be moved, but one of our nursing staff discovered on her early-morning round that your aunt had so sadly, and unexpectedly, passed peacefully away in her sleep during the night. Please accept our sincerest condolences. As one of the long-term residents, your great-aunt was a great favourite and will be sadly missed."

Kirsten, although shocked, regained her composure. "Thank you, for all that you and your staff have done for Kathryn over the years. It is much appreciated."

"And thank you for those kind comments." The caller paused. "If it's not too inappropriate, could I ask that either you or your father please attend the hospital at the first opportunity? There are, obviously, as I am sure you will understand, some unfortunate but necessary arrangements to be made." Kirsten thanked the caller and put the phone down. She would make all the necessary arrangements; her stepmother would have no problem with that.

*

This visit was the complete opposite of her last, which, after the awkward minutes of her initial arrival, was full of joy and fond memories. She was ushered into a side office and introduced to a Mr Pengelly, the nurse manager, who asked her if she would like a tea or coffee, which she politely refused. A cardboard file was produced, which, by the look of it, had not seen the light of day for many a year.

"I don't quite know how to say this but in regard to your great-aunt, there appears to be in place an extremely long-term covenant between the hospital and a third party, which covers everything to do with any arrangements required in the event of her demise."

Kirsten was bemused. "Could I enquire as to who this third party is?"

"I'm afraid I cannot say. The covenant expressly forbids the disclosure and anyway it is not shown in these documents. However, I have checked with the finance department and, as it states, the funding is definitely there in a separate dedicated account, having been invested over an extremely long period of time." Kirsten enquired as to what specific arrangements had been made and was informed it included everything from the location of the churchyard burial plot, which had been purchased decades ago, to the cost of an undertaker and church service.

"Could I ask where this burial plot is located?"

"Of course, as I remember from the text, it is at the church of St Mary's in the small village of Little Filbraham on the Cambridgeshire Suffolk border, not far from here actually. If you just wait a minute, I will print you off the relevant details." This he did whilst still talking to Kirsten. "And there is one other thing…" he paused, "…by the side of her bed we discovered these, which had been neatly placed on the bedside table." So saying, he produced a folded note and a small, very old biscuit tin which he slid across the desk.

"And what does the note say?"

"Please, I think you must read it yourself."

She picked up the note which was simply addressed:

To Kirsten,
These are for you. Please keep the memories they contain in
your heart.

With tears forming in her eyes, she managed to get out, "Do you know what the tin box contains?"

"I'm afraid not. We thought it too personal to look. Maybe you should open it when you are alone and in private." Kirsten brushed the tears away, nodded her agreement and let it be known that after due consideration, she was of the opinion that the wishes of the covenant should be honoured, that is, if the contents were in accordance with all that was required and appropriate. Of course, once a funeral director had been appointed, she would very much like to discuss the details of any arrangements and dates, etc. Mr Pengelly agreed and said he would put the affair in the hands of the stated trustees, who would most certainly be contacting her in the next few days. After some more small talk, Kirsten picked up the box and note, said thank you to the manager for all that the hospital had done and was still doing for her great-aunt and then left.

That night, Kirsten poured herself a glass of red wine, put on her favourite Oscar Peterson album and curled up on the couch. In front of her on the coffee table was the note and biscuit tin. She picked up the note, read it one more time, carefully folded it and placed it down again. She considered the small metal tin for a moment. Was this all that remained of her great-aunt's eighty years on this earth? Slowly, she lifted up the tin and carefully removed the lid. It was almost empty and one by one she removed the meagre contents and placed them side by side on the table. A 1935 silver dollar, a pressed ear of wheat mounted on cardboard, a lock of jet-black hair in a tiny box, a folded handwritten receipt and a photograph of three children: two boys and a girl. She picked up the photograph, which for its age was remarkably sharp and showed little sign of fading. The girl in the centre was obviously Kathryn and there was no denying that, but who were the two boys?

*

Kirsten, dressed in black with her father by her side, stood next to the grave. The service, although short, was beautiful in its simplicity. The village choir had sung *Abide with Me* and she had spoken a few words about Kathryn, necessarily short, as in truth, she knew very little about her great-aunt's early life. Her mother had first taken her to see her great-aunt when she, Kirsten, was just a toddler, and her memories of those visits were, to say the least, cloudy. That would be twenty-five or more years ago, and Kathryn would already have been in her fifties. Even after the loss of her mother, she had kept her great-aunt's memory close and as soon as she was old enough and independent, she had made the occasional visit to the hospital, thus defying her stepmother, who had done her utmost to expunge Kathryn's name from the family history.

As the coffin was slowly lowered into its final resting place and the threatened rain in the form of light drizzle materialised, Kirsten glanced up, looking around at the twenty plus mourners all dressed in black who had gathered at the grave. A similar thought now went through her mind to the one that had occurred fifteen minutes earlier as she read the address from the lectern in the church. Who were these people? She knew none of them. Most of them were obviously elderly and, apart from her father, none of them family.

As the vicar gave his closing words, she looked straight past him at a tall man dressed in a trench coat standing well back next to a high headstone. As she watched, he turned and spoke to another figure who was standing at his side and who, on first impressions, appeared to be the complete opposite of the younger man, being slightly hunched and so poorly dressed that he gave all the appearance of being an elderly tramp.

She was brought back to reality by her father, who was letting her know that he would be on his way directly. "But I have not organised anything for all these people."

Her father turned around and then turned back again. "Well, it doesn't look like that will be too much of a problem, as most of them seem to have disappeared!" He left Kirsten at the graveside and went over to the vicar, thanked him for the service and returned, gave Kirsten a quick kiss on the cheek and left. Kirsten walked slowly across to join the vicar, who was now standing by the church door. "Thank you, Reverend. I believe we gave her the simple but fitting send-off she would have wanted… but something is tormenting me… maybe you can help."

"If I can help, I will only be too pleased to do so."

"In all honesty, I have to say, that obviously apart from my father, I didn't recognise any of the mourners. I can only assume they were local village people who had known her in her youth!"

"That is absolutely amazing. I was only thinking a similar thing myself. I thought these people must be relatives, as I did not recognise any of them, but having said that, I have only been the vicar here for five years, so I cannot say with absolute certainty… although I do try my best… who is local and who is not!"

"There was one person, quite young, probably in his early twenties, I would say, and dressed in a trench coat. He was stood well back over there by the tall headstone, sheltering under the yew tree."

"I'm so sorry. Funerals do attract some strange people, just an inquisitive passer-by maybe!"

"And the tramp, he spoke to the tramp."

"Ah, now maybe I can help you there. Was he slightly hunched and walked with a pronounced limp?"

"I cannot comment on the limp but the rest fits."

"Yes, well, that will be Michael. He works for me, a sort of occasional part-time handyman. He shouldn't really still be doing manual work at his age, but he's as honest as the day is long and totally reliable."

Kirsten made a mental note of what the vicar had said, thanked him, turned and walked slowly back to her car.

TEN

THE DISCOVERY

As the Bard said, '*When sorrows come, they come not as single spies, but in battalions*', but is that also true of more pleasing news?

The next morning, the day after the funeral, her attention was attracted by the post, which dropped through the letterbox with a heavier-than-usual clunk. There on the door mat, amongst the usual array of inconsequential dross, was a small neatly packed parcel, which she picked up and took to the kitchen diner. Turning it over, she noticed it was from Cherry Wood Hall. Intrigued, she carefully opened it. Inside was a small old-fashioned photograph album and a short note from Mr Pengelly:

Dear Miss Davies,

I'm sure you will be interested in this small photograph album which was discovered when Apple Tree Ward was being cleared by the developers. One of the workmen was good enough to bring it to my office. It was found at the back of your great-aunt's side cupboard and had obviously slipped down behind one of the drawers, probably been there for years.

Anyway, I thought you may like it.

If I can be of any help in the future, please do not hesitate to contact me.

Yours faithfully,
E.H. Pengelly
Nurse Manager

Kirsten made herself a coffee and took the album into her lounge and sat in the sunlight under the window. It was definitely her aunt's and contained a treasure trove of family memories. Not only were there photographs of Kathryn as a child and teenager but also images of her mother and father and what appeared to be two brothers. Some of the black and white photographs were so faded that it was only just possible to make out a barely discernible outline, whilst others, like the sepia-tinted examples, looked like they had been printed only yesterday. Sadly, the album was only half full, but the biggest surprise came with the very last print. It was a photograph of a pilot kneeling on the wing of a World War Two fighter, fully suited up in his flying gear, helmet, boots and life jacket, looking very relaxed with his arm around a large black dog. Trying hard, she searched for detail, but the helmet, goggles and oxygen mask hid most of his hair and a lot of his face. Who was this man? Was it just a teenage heart-throb or someone Kathryn had really known?

She carefully pulled it out and turned it over. It was clearly marked *The Army Film and Photographic Unit* (AFPU).

Kirsten leaned back, contemplating this new discovery. For the first time in her life, she now had evidence, albeit tenuous, of the possibility of undiscovered family members, and also, and most intriguingly, who was this pilot?

The reasons for the slimness of her family tree were obvious. First of all, her father was an only child and both of his parents had passed on many years ago. The single entry on her mother's side was down to the simple fact that her mother had been adopted as a very young baby. However, like Kirsten, she too had wanted to know more about her family and through many hours of searching had found Great-Aunt Kathryn but that was all. Who could help her in this quest to broaden her family tree? She wouldn't know where to start.

Of course, the answer was obvious: William Benjamin, the researcher and writer. The words were still there in her memory: *Miss, if in the future you ever need help on any subject to do with the history of Cherry Wood Hall, please do not hesitate to call me on this number.* She paused, frantically trying to remember. What did she do with that card? A short search produced the card, which was still there in the pocket of her summer jacket, and within minutes she was on the phone to William Benjamin.

"Mr Benjamin, this is Kirsten Davies—"

She was just about to go on to say that they had met at Cherry Wood Hall, when he interrupted. "Ah, the lady on the steps, I was half expecting a call from you."

Kirsten was taken aback. "Excuse me, how did you know my name?"

"No outstanding reason really. I'm just quite good at recognising voices."

"Oh, I see, and why would you be expecting a call from me?"

"Easy, you see, I have had the run of that wing of the hospital for the last few weeks, up and down those steps to the archives in the cellar so many times, and I was well aware that Miss Kathryn was the last remaining patient in Apple Tree Ward, which as you know was a special ward, and you did tell me you were visiting your great-aunt, who was a patient there."

"Quite true, I hope I don't appear rude, but I must say you are quite a detective."

"Well, I've found out that when writing a factual book, research is everything, and the more you look, the more you discover, but what can I do for you?" Kirsten went on to describe the events of the last week or two and the photographs. "I'm so sorry to hear about the death of your great-aunt. She was the last of a long line in that ward but, please, how can I be of further help?"

"Mr Benjamin, the way you have talked of access to archives, etc., can I assume that your project has some degree of official backing?"

"That is indeed true."

"Well, what I would dearly love to know is, are there any details that relate to the names and/or addresses of my great-aunt's family? You see, I am trying to get a fuller understanding of my family tree."

"Miss Davies, well, you are quite correct in one aspect and that I have copies of all patient admission records going back seventy years, but I do have to warn you, sometimes I may uncover details which are, how can I say this, not always palatable or pleasing to an enquiring relative."

"I understand but that's fine with me. I'm sure most families have a skeleton in the cupboard somewhere along the line."

"Right then, please leave it with me. I will see what background details I can find on Kathryn Alexander and get back to you as soon as I have anything."

Kirsten put the phone down. At least she had now got the ball rolling, but enough of this. There was a real world out there and she was a professional commercial pilot. She got up, went across to her flight bag and opened it, took out the *Boeing 737NG Flight Manual* and decided to find out if she was still as sharp as she was before her accident. Halfway through *Operation with a Single Generator*, the phone went. "Gracious, this man is quick." But it wasn't William Benjamin at all; it was a voice from her not-too-distant past. It was Ven Carlson. For reasons she could not explain, it was impossible for her to hide the obvious pleasure she took in hearing his voice.

"Ven, so good to hear from you again. What time is it with you? It's only 11:30 am here and if you are in Arizona, it must be the middle of the night."

"Well, that's where you're mistaken. You see, I'm in Boston and just about to board an all-expenses-paid international flight, albeit on an airline I have to say I have never heard of."

"Lucky you. Somewhere exotic and first class, I hope!"

"Well, if you call somewhere called Stansted exotic, I guess it is, and as for first class, why, that's reserved for off-duty flight crew, isn't it?"

Kirsten laughed but ignored the last remark. "You're coming here. I can show you around. Is it for long?"

"Well, remember sometime back, I told you about the occasional requests I get to guest fly Mustangs at air shows, well, that's what I'm doing. I've added a few days on either side of the big Cambridge weekend show, so I'll have some time to spare and it would be great to meet up again."

"Where will you be staying?"

"For the first night, I'll be staying in the airport hotel and then it will be up to me. I guess a place close to the display field would suit, but I can sort that out tomorrow."

"Tell you what. I'm not too far away. I'll pick you up in the foyer of the airport hotel at ten. That will give you time to eat your free breakfast."

They talked about the latest events for a couple of minutes but then, in the background, Kirsten heard the announcement for, "*Final call for flight 335 to London Stansted, England.*"

"That's your final call. You had better go... See you tomorrow."

"Still as bossy as ever... See you then."

Kirsten smiled and put the receiver down. It wasn't much but life had taken a small turn for the better.

*

Things went according to plan and there was Ven, standing outside the main hotel entrance, a suitcase in one hand and half-eaten piece of toast in the other. He walked round to the rear of the car and placed the case in the boot before clambering in beside her.

"Nice wheels, sorry about the crumbs." Kirsten ignored the crumbs remark.

"Well, it's my only extravagance. I get paid well and why shouldn't I enjoy the fruits of my labours?"

"Labour? I thought you flew for the love of it."

"Same old Ven, sharp as ever. Good to see you haven't changed."

"Sorry, Kirsten, I was forgetting you were my equal in a verbal sparring match... like the new short hairstyle, by the way."

She laughed and turned the car onto the M11 motorway. "Duxford is only about 20 miles from here."

"Well, I'm completely in your hands. Is there a decent motel nearby?"

Kirsten explained that Cambridge was a bit thin on motels but there was a decent old-fashioned hotel in Sawford which was almost within walking distance of the airfield. She spent the rest of the journey explaining the events of the last few weeks, with Ven politely listening. Kirsten parked in the hotel carpark and turned to Ven. "I've stayed here myself. It's kind of old school but comfortable. The food is good and I took the liberty of booking a room for you."

"Sounds perfect, I'll check in." He paused but then went on, "Are you doing anything special for the rest of the day?"

"Well, you know that researcher writer I told you about earlier, William Benjamin, I got a call from him earlier this morning. Apparently, he has some information on my Great-Aunt Kathryn, and it's kind of delicate in nature. He says what he has found out is not suitable for delivering over the phone, whatever that means, so I am on my way to see him. Ironically, he lives not far from where we have just buried her."

"That sounds kind of personal."

"Not really, please feel free to tag along. She spent most of her life in a mental institution, so whatever he has to say can't be too shocking."

"OK, just give me fifteen minutes and I'll be right with you," and so saying, he disappeared into the hotel.

Kirsten sat there, reflecting. Was she turning this whole Aunt Kathryn thing into an unnatural obsession? Ven returned and without thinking went to the right-hand side of the car and placed his hand on the door handle. "Thinking of driving, Mr Carlson?"

"Sorry, must still be jet-lagged, but I'll never work out why most of Europe drives on the right but you Brits insist on driving on the other side."

"Well, there is a reason but it's complicated. Maybe we will save it for another day."

Ven made himself comfortable and fastened his seat belt. "Take it away, Miss Davies."

On the way, Kirsten mentioned that she was not due to meet Mr Williams until two thirty that afternoon, so maybe they could take lunch at a decent-looking pub she had spotted in Little Filbraham on the day of her aunt's funeral. "Sounds good to me."

The car park of the Dog and Duck was full, but the strange thing was that most of the vehicles were old American Army vehicles, ranging from Jeeps to two GMC 6x6s which were parked out in the street. Ven undid his seat belt and craned his neck to get a better view.

"Wow, what's going on here?"

"I have no idea, hope they still have a table free."

"Why, did you book one?"

"Of course I did."

"Well, that's really nice of you… but I'm not sure what it means. Either I'm totally predictable or a sucker for a free lunch." Ven closed his eyes; once again, he had just put his foot firmly in his mouth!

But Kirsten had an answer as she got out of the car: "Hey, who says I'm paying!"

Ven laughed. "Fair enough, let's go then."

The pub was full of characters all dressed in American service uniform or fatigues, mainly seated around two refectory tables. Ven paused at the door. "Looks like we have gate-crashed a party. Maybe we should look somewhere else."

"Strange, the gentleman who took my table booking made no mention of this!"

A waitress appeared at Kirsten's side. "Would it be Miss Davies plus one?" Kirsten nodded. "Please take a seat at the bar. Your table, which is in the snug round the corner from the bar, will be free in a few minutes."

The barman, who also looked like he was the landlord, gave them a friendly greeting. "What can I get you?"

Kirsten ordered a fruit juice, as she was driving, and, when Ven asked what she would recommend for him, suggested he try English bitter. Ven, who had seen a few English films of country life, requested in a jocular way, "A pint of your Best Bitter, please, landlord," to which the landlord with a perfectly straight face replied, "All my bitter is best, sir."

Ven, now completely nonplussed and not knowing what to say next, turned to Kirsten for help, but the landlord, who was now wearing a broad grin, helped him out. "My apologies, sir, I just couldn't resist it. You see, English pubs stopped marketing what was known as Best Bitter years ago."

Ven put his hands up whilst glancing along the back of the bar. "OK, I surrender. I see something there called a guest beer. I'll have a pint of that, please."

The noise from the large party group was quite loud and Ven enquired, "Who are these people? Sounds like they are enjoying themselves," to which the landlord replied that they were a re-enact group who took a fortnight out every year, going round the local air-shows, and that they always made a point of having at least one lunch in the Dog and Duck. Apparently, they took it all very seriously and had been up at the old US Linton Grange airfield practising that very morning. "Mike the Mint smooths the way for them, as he lives up there."

Ven was intrigued. "Mike the Mint, he sounds quite a character."

"Sure, Mike has been around for as long as I can remember. When we were kids growing up, we used to torment him something rotten. Basically, he is an old tramp who used to push his dog around in an ancient pushchair. He has a gammy leg, so he could never catch us."

Kirsten looked up from her fruit juice. "Would this be the same man who does odd work for the vicar, like cutting grass and digging graves?"

"That's him. Sounds like you have already met him."

"Not actually met him, but I did see him at my aunt's funeral a few days ago."

The landlord nodded. "If you talk to him, the first thing you will notice is that although he has been here for as long as most people can remember, he still has this strong American accent."

Ven interjected. "Incredible, can't be too many US hobos over here."

The landlord agreed. "There are lots of stories explaining how he got here, and you never know which one to believe, but the most common one is that he was a young US serviceman from World War Two who got romantically linked to some local woman and never went back. Anyway, he lives rough in one of the old huts up there."

Ven did know a little about the war and was genuinely interested. "Linton Grange, that was an 8th Air Force fighter station, wasn't it? I would sure like to take a wander round the old base. Is it accessible?"

"Well, it is and it isn't, if you know what I mean. It's not a question of legal access or anything like that, it's more a question of... How can I say this? People feel uncomfortable up there."

Kirsten was listening. "I'm sorry, what do you mean uncomfortable?"

"Well, for instance, over the years, in order to make the wheat-growing and harvesting easier, the owners have tried to have a lot of the concrete taxiways dug up but, and I think this has happened three times now, whoever is contracted to do it runs into trouble."

"What sort of trouble?"

"Well, they move in with their JCBs but never last more than a day. The workmen just refuse to carry on or go any further. One of the drivers jumped out of his machine and didn't stop running until he was halfway here."

"Good grief, what frightens them?"

"All sorts: weird noises, voices, invisible hands on shoulders, you name it... and it has now got to the point where no local company will go anywhere near the place."

Ven was really interested. "But Mike the Mint lives up there!"

"Sure, that's the strange thing, he does and anyone can go there and wander round. It's only if you try and disturb things that this stuff happens. As kids, we cycled up there and tried to dig up some lead from the machine gun sand buts. Well, we lasted about five minutes and this enormous German Shepherd guard dog appeared and chased us off."

"Well, surely it was only doing what it was supposed to do!"

"Right, but that's the thing, the farmer who owned the place didn't have a German Shepherd dog!" The barman moved away to serve another customer.

Ven and Kirsten looked at each other, both deep in their own thoughts.

"What's the beer like?"

"Very good, quite strong, maybe just a little warm."

The waitress was back again. "Your table is ready, if you would like to follow me. Please bring your drinks with you."

Seated at their table in the snug, they discovered, after glancing around them, that they were the only diners in there. The waitress had left two lunchtime menus and pointed out the specials on an old blackboard hung above the fireplace. "Doesn't get much more English than this. Real cosy, as you might say." Ven glanced down at the menu and then across at the specials board. "If it's anything like the States, the specials are usually good value."

Kirsten looked up, absentmindedly. She was still thinking about Mike the Mint. "Sure, we are not far from the coast here, so the sea bass would probably be a good choice."

"Suits me."

The waitress returned. "Are you ready to order?"

"Two sea bass, please, and if you could, another pint of this when you have a moment." The waitress disappeared with their order but was soon back with Ven's beer.

"Could I bring a jug of water with your meal, madam?"

Kirsten replied, "Terrific – thank you."

The fish arrived and it lived up to all expectations. They ate slowly whilst exchanging various viewpoints on this and that. Kirsten looked at her watch. "We better think about making a move, I'll go and settle up."

Ven protested but was firmly put in his place. "My invitation, so it's on me. Just drink up, we must be going." She got up and disappeared round the corner to the bar. Sitting there, Ven was conscious that something had changed. What was it? Got it, no noise, the re-enactors had left, but then a shape appeared in the snug doorway and made its way towards him. It was a tall young man, immaculately dressed in the pinks and greens of a USAAF pilot of WW2.

Ven was impressed. "You are a credit to the people you remember, sir."

The stranger stopped and turned towards him and then replied in a strong New York accent. "Why, thank you. Going by your accent, you must be an American. Am I correct?"

"Certainly am. I am over here for the air-show next weekend. I fly P-51 Mustangs." The stranger's face brightened. "Maybe we have something in common, sir."

"I would offer you a seat and a beer, but my lady friend will be back soon and this table is quite small."

"No problem, I'm on my way out." So saying, he bade farewell.

"Good to meet you, sir," and he continued on his way.

Ven got up to join Kirsten, who was at the till, chatting to the landlord. He waited for a small break in their conversation and then, leaning over Kirsten's shoulder, made a throwaway comment. "I must say, some of those re-enactor guys are dressed immaculately. The one I have just been speaking to looked like he had been dressed by a tailor."

The landlord looked up, his face bearing an inquisitive look. "But they all left fifteen minutes ago, and as I remember, to a man, they were dressed in working dress or fatigues."

"Well, this one wasn't. He was in full dress uniform."

"Where is he now?"

"Well, back there somewhere. Maybe he left by the back door."

"There hasn't been a back door for fifty years, not since they built the extension in the fifties." The three of them looked at each other and then in one movement stepped into the snug – it was empty!

*

They sat in the BMW, with Kirsten trying to console Ven. "Am I going nuts? Why is it, Kirsten, these crazy things only happen when I'm with you? Sorry, I didn't mean anything by that, but I really did see that guy, you know!"

"Don't worry. There will be an explanation. We just don't know what it is." She decided to change the subject.

"Damn, I meant to bring that photo of the pilot along with me to show you. If he was in any way well known, why, with your Mustang background knowledge, I'm sure you would have recognised him straight away."

Ven was calm again. "Maybe, but I only know a few of them. Can you see much of the aeroplane? Sometimes, it's easier to identify the pilot by his aeroplane – hang on, thinking about it, do you have any contacts in the local vintage military warbird community? Some of those guys have detailed knowledge you wouldn't believe."

"Not really, my pilot friends are mostly into competition aerobatics." She hesitated. "But of course there is Roger Deacon. He's got a foot in both camps."

"Try him. If he doesn't know, he probably knows someone who does."

"OK, I'll try him tonight, but we must get going if we are going to get to the Benjamin place by two thirty."

Kirsten set off down the high street, at the end of which she forked left down a narrow country lane. "Hope we don't meet a farm tractor coming the other way, don't fancy reversing half a mile back up here," to which Ven replied, "Don't worry, leave any talking to me, ma'am. By the way, where are we looking for?"

Kirsten frowned and looked at him, remarking that he had had only two pints of strong bitter, then proceeded to pull a piece of paper from the glovebox and handed it across. "Manor House, back road, Little Filbraham... what sort of Zip is that? Haven't you people discovered blocks and street numbers yet?"

"The instructions are clear enough. Turn off down the lane at the end of the high street and continue for about half a mile, which, according to my calculations, is about here... and thére it is!" She parked in the quite spacious drive and they both got out.

Ven was still in a playful mood. "Will we be having afternoon tea and cakes, do you think?"

"Behave yourself. We, well, at least I, am here on serious business." Ven waggled his head in mock disbelief.

There was no need to ring the doorbell. William Benjamin had seen them coming; the front door was already open and he was standing there with his wife by his side. "Mr and… I assume Mrs Benjamin, so good to see you. This is a close friend of mine, Mr Ven Carlson."

They shook hands and were led into a large study where they were seated next to a small table. At this point, Mrs Benjamin declared, "Tea, everyone," and, so saying, departed to put the kettle on.

"I understand you have unearthed some history regarding my Great-Aunt Kathryn Alexander, something which could expand my family tree knowledge. However, I gather some of it may be a little sensitive!"

"Well, it certainly is that. Can I speak freely in front of Mr Carlson?"

"But of course." Kirsten turned to Ven, who smiled appropriately.

William Benjamin started to pick his words carefully, explaining that he himself was a foundling who had spent many years trying to establish his parentage, and did they know what a foundling was? Kirsten replied that she had not really given it much thought but assumed it was similar to an orphan, and didn't they used to have foundling hospitals?

"There were indeed and I myself am a product of one of those." But, of course, he explained, "The parents of an orphan are known but sadly deceased, whereas the parents of a foundling are unknown."

"Are you saying my Great-Aunt Kathryn was a foundling?"

"No, I'm afraid not. It's far, far more complex than that. I think the best way to explain this is with the documents I have unearthed." He got up, went across to his bureau and removed a large brown envelope, placing it on the table. He then proceeded to remove the documents it contained.

"As you can see from this one, your aunt was committed to Cherry Wood on the 18th of November 1944, under the Mental Deficiency Act of 1913."

He paused again but was interrupted by Kirsten. "And what is the significance in that?"

"It was... and I will quote the act verbatim, '*The Mental Deficiency Act of 1913* was an act of Parliament of the United Kingdom which made provisions for the institutional treatment of people deemed to be *feeble minded* and *morally defective.*'"

Kirsten was puzzled. "I'm sorry, I don't follow."

William Benjamin paused. "There is no other way to say this, and the admission documents clearly state it." He paused again. "Your great-aunt was deemed to be morally defective, in that she was pregnant with child and unmarried, which meant she was considered by her parents, as shown in their written statement, to be feeble of mind and incapable of correct moral choices."

The anger swelled up within Kirsten. "Are you telling me my Great-Aunt Kathryn was placed in a mental institution for no other reason than that she had an illegitimate child?"

Ven reached out and placed a comforting hand on hers, but there was nothing he could say.

William Benjamin did not know what to say either. "Would you like me to continue?"

"Yes, I would very much like that."

"The documents are extremely unusual in that they contain several annotated and signed alterations and additions. Would you like to see them?"

"I would indeed."

William Benjamin spread out the admission documents. "Here, you can see that the address of the parents, which was originally the village of Lintock, has been changed to an address in the village of Little Filbraham, just up the road, of course."

"Would there be a reason for that?"

"Probably down to one simple thing... and that is, I hate to say it... and that would be... shame."

Kirsten nodded. "So they moved, but please go on."

"There is another thing which is very hard to understand, and that is, the parents' surname is given as Collins, but an instruction is given to the hospital that the patient should be known not by her christened name of Rose but by her aunt's name of Kathryn and her grandmother's maiden surname of Alexander."

"So my Great-Aunt Kathryn Alexander was really Great-Aunt Rose Collins."

Benjamin nodded. "But there is more."

Kirsten interjected. "Of course, the child. What happened to the child?"

"Exactly, and this is probably the most important piece of the puzzle." He waited, looking for an element of confirmation in Kirsten's eyes before continuing.

"The child, a female child, was put up for adoption and she was adopted by a couple by the name of..." he hesitated once again, "...a Mr and Mrs Eddington."

Kirsten jerked back, which took Ven completely by surprise. "What's so shocking about the name Eddington?"

Kirsten took in a deep breath and sat back in her chair. "Eddington was my mother's maiden name! My mother hadn't found her aunt… she'd found her mother… my grandmother!"

The silence was broken by Mrs Benjamin. "Who is for tea and cakes then?"

ELEVEN

THE BROTHERS IN ARMS

Once back in the car, Kirsten sat reflecting. "Well, that was a turn-up for the book. It's going to take a while before it all sinks in."

Ven was more positive. "I think it's good news. You now have an uninterrupted bloodline going back several generations."

Kirsten shrugged her shoulders and indicated a tacit agreement with a nod of her head. "But, Ven, it's made me even more determined to solve the riddle of the contents of the tin box and those photographs."

Ven had been giving it some thought as well. "Tell you what, as we are so close, why don't we take a trip up to the old Linton Grange Air Base? Personally, I would like that."

Kirsten could not help but show a little guilt. "Of course, Ven, I'm supposed to be showing you around, aren't I? I've been totally selfish, so yea, let's do it." She placed the key in the ignition but hesitated and turned again to Ven. "Just before we go, would you mind if we make a quick visit to the churchyard? I have some fresh flowers in the back."

The vicar of St Mary's caught them as they were going in. Kirsten stopped, only wishing to exchange pleasantries. "Miss Davies, so good to see you again. By the way, I did a little more enquiring as regards your question about the mourners at your great-aunt's funeral."

Kirsten turned. "Ah, Vicar, this is a close friend of mine, Mr Ven Carlson." The vicar shook Ven's hand and Kirsten continued... "Did your enquiries throw any light on the mystery?"

"Strangely, no, I asked the choir master and the organist, both of whom have lived here a lifetime, and neither of them recognised anyone apart from Mike, the handyman... It is most strange."

"It is indeed. By the way, if you see Mike, I would be grateful if you could ask if he knew any of them."

"I will indeed, he is due to cut the grass on Wednesday. I'll be out visiting most of the day but will be back by late afternoon. It's an all-day job so I should catch him before he finishes." Kirsten thanked the reverend and indicated she was on her way to place some fresh flowers on the grave, and so saying, they parted.

She was in the act of changing the flowers when Ven, who was loitering slightly to one side of the grave, called her across. "Kirsten, I think there is something here you should take a look at!" Bending down on one knee, he was intently looking at the headstone of the grave next door. Kirsten knelt by his side and read the inscription.

IN LOVING MEMORY OF
JANE COLLINS 1901–1972
AND JACK COLLINS 1896–1962,
MOTHER AND FATHER OF TWO LOVING SONS,
WHO GAVE THEIR LIVES IN THE
1939–1945 CONFLICT,
AND A LONG-LOST DAUGHTER

Kirsten stood erect between the two graves. "Of course, how stupid of me, the obvious benefactor of the plot would have been one or both of her parents, and where better than right next door to their own, and neither the church, nor myself for that matter, would have connected the name Collins with Alexander."

Ven placed his arm gently around her shoulder. "Well, it's something you can certainly put right when it comes to the new grave headstone… and I tell you something else…" Kirsten gave him an enquiring look. "…you know you said one or both, my money's on her mother… mothers don't put their daughters in mental institutions just for getting in the family way." Kirsten nodded; that made good sense.

The BMW crunched into the gravel which led onto a wide concrete surfaced area just off the road. "Dispersal pan if you ask me. Maybe we should park and walk from here."

The old airbase didn't show much obvious evidence of its history apart from the two large hangars in the distance, which looked like they were now part of some industrial site, and the remains of the control tower, which was rapidly being consumed by shrubby vegetation. "It's just like the landlord of the pub said. The taxiways look hardly touched, must be a real pain in the butt at ploughing time."

Kirsten was examining some strange form of bushy brown vegetation which appeared to be growing between each concrete section of the taxiway. "What on earth is this? Never seen anything like it before."

"Me neither, it's almost like some form of tumbleweed, and it only grows between the concrete sections, very strange. The old place really seems to have atmosphere. You can just imagine P-51s roaring off down one of the three runways."

Ven closed his eyes and listened but there was nothing. "I guess the prevailing wind is from the east, so the main runway would have been... dead in front of us."

Kirsten was connecting well with his chain of thought. "That makes total sense and would be the reason why the control tower is where it is. Let's walk on." In a hundred yards, they came to a junction where the taxiway split, carrying straight on with a spur turning off to the left. Ven crossed over to the ploughed edge to investigate a large lump of rusty iron that was partially covered with vine weed. "Would you believe it's an old plough?"

Kirsten laughed. "Horse or tractor-pulled?"

"I'm no expert but I would say tractor." He had hardly completed the sentence when they were both surprised and shocked by the barking of a dog, which was definitely getting closer.

Together, they both thought, *German Shepherd!* A very vocal and large black and white Border Collie was streaking towards them. Kirsten uttered what Ven was thinking: "I hope he stops bloody soon."

Ven, who knew a little about dogs, took her hand and reassured her. "Just stay still and calm. It's only a Collie, for Christ's sake." The dog came to a sliding halt just in front of them and then proceeded to go down on his belly, furiously wagging his tail. Ven offered an outstretched hand to the Collie, which was immediately back on his feet. "What's up, boy? Are you lost?" He looked up and around but there was nobody in sight on the flat open old airfield. The dog turned and started slowly walking away, only to stop and turn his head, panting, whilst lolling his massive tongue. "Do you want us to follow you, is that it?" The dog took a few paces forward and stopped again.

Kirsten was convinced. "That's exactly what he wants." They followed the Collie for ten minutes, during which time he took them along the track that curved around the remains of an old airfield Maycrete structure and then on towards more buildings that were partially hidden by clumps of ubiquitous silver birch trees. "Where's he taking us? Hope nobody's in trouble. Sometimes, these old airfield structures can be quite unsafe after sixty years of neglect." Kirsten was expressing her concerns.

Ven paused and answered, "You know, I think this is the original domestic site, appears to be a mixture of old Quonset and Nissen huts, some of which are being used for pig pens by the smell of it." At that moment, the dog disappeared down a left turn. "Where's he going now?"

On turning the corner, the answer became clear, twenty yards along the track. Ven, who was a few paces ahead, stopped and pointed. "Would you believe this!" There on the right was a short-sized Nissen hut, which had withstood the ravages of time, as someone, probably the farmer, had taken the trouble to give it a skin of fibreglass plus a thick coat of green paint. The windows were all intact and, what was strangest of all, the tall, thin smoke stack was emitting wisps of pale blue smoke from under its conical lid. Their friend the Collie was stretched out on the front doorstep, next to an old Raleigh bicycle that was propped up under a window. They both stood there, wondering what to do next.

Their dream-like state was interrupted by a low, strange voice with a distinct American twang that came from behind them. "Can I help you people?"

Turning, they were confronted by Mike the Mint, who was carrying a bundle of firewood under his arm. Ven just told it as it was. "We were just looking over the old air base and your dog, Rover," he pointed at the Collie, "kind of got our attention and led us here."

"He's not my dog, belongs to the farmer on the other side of the base."

"So why did he lead us here?"

"Well, he often takes it into his head to come and spend a day with me, the farmer doesn't seem to mind… and as you have just found out, he also decides now and again that I need some company."

Ven went across and tousled the Collie's ears. "What a great dog, what's his name?"

"Well, I call him Laddie. He seems to answer to that."

Kirsten, who had been holding back, taking everything in, then stepped forward. "Would I be correct in assuming you must live here, sir?"

"For more years than I can remember, but I would not change it. You see, I am at peace with the world here."

"Something we all strive for... By the way, I'm Kirsten Davies and this is a good friend of mine, Ven Carlson."

Mike was quick to answer. "Oh, I know who you are, Miss Davies." He left his answer short of any explanation but went on, "Everyone calls me Mike. Can I invite you in for a cup of tea?"

This placed Kirsten and Ven in a bit of a dilemma, as they had been drinking tea all afternoon, but good manners dictated Kirsten's answer. "That's very kind of you. We would love to come in but... might pass on the tea." Mike opened the front door and led them in. The interior was tidy and neat but reeked of the smell of woodsmoke originating from the pot-bellied stove in the centre of the single room, a stove that he obviously used for heating and cooking.

"Please excuse the stove, same as it ever was, freezing in winter, sweltering in summer... By the way, I'm due over at the farm in ten minutes so I can't stay long. How can I help you?"

Kirsten got the impression that he already knew what she wanted. "It's about my great-aunt's funeral."

"Great-aunt, is it? Well..." he hesitated, "...it's quite complicated but there is an easy way to explain things."

"And please what would that be?"

"Just this... be here at zero four hundred hours this coming Thursday morning and all will be made perfectly clear... and... I must be going now. As I said, I must be over the other side, I have a job to do." With this, he disappeared out of the door, with a bemused Kirsten and Ven following close behind.

Ven could not resist a parting shot. "Zero four hundred hours, that's the middle of the night."

Without turning, Mike gave a quick reply. "Where have I heard that before?"

Within seconds, he was disappearing into the distance on his bicycle, with the Collie trotting along beside him.

The journey back to the hotel was spent questioning the day's events and planning the next few days. "Ven, I know this is a bit of an imposition, but how are you fixed for the rest of the week, especially Thursday?"

"Well, I have a full briefing and a meeting with the Mustang's owner tomorrow, that'll be Tuesday taken care of. Wednesday, I'll be free."

"How about Thursday? You wouldn't let a poor vulnerable female wander about a deserted airfield on her own at four in the morning, would you?" She turned and cheekily fluttered her eyelashes at him.

"Have you no shame, woman? Well, actually, I have a first practice after lunch, but I should be free during the morning and I'll have a set of hire car wheels by then, so transport is not a problem."

Kirsten was considering Mike's words. "What's he going to show or tell us on Thursday that he could not have told us today?"

"Beats me, but something is telling me it's going to involve his re-enactor friends."

"But why four in the morning?" All Ven could do was shrug his shoulders and remind her to phone Roger Deacon that evening.

Kirsten dropped Ven off at his hotel, wished him good luck for the next day and let him know she would phone him at the hotel the following evening.

She arrived back at her flat, parked her car and let herself in. Sitting down on the couch, she gave free flow to her thoughts. The truth was, in one day, she had discovered more about her mother's family than she had managed in the whole of the rest of her life to date. On the other hand, it had generated so many unanswered questions, and something else was troubling her: did her father know the truth about her grandmother's identity? There again, was it important? Would revealing her discovery to him only stir up more trouble? Things were bad enough between her and her stepmother; telling them would only make things worse. So, what should she do next? She must phone Roger Deacon before it got too late, but first things first: were there any eggs in the fridge? She could kill an omelette.

"Hello, Roger. Long time, no see. It's Kirsten Davies here."

"Kirsten, good to hear from you. I heard about your accident. Are you OK now?"

"About ninety-nine per cent. I have a small problem with my left eye, but the doc is confident that will clear up in the next week or two. Meanwhile I'm enjoying some time off, doing a bit of research, you might say."

"It probably wouldn't shock you to know that the whole Warbird community has taken to checking their canopy rails before they fly. You were so unlucky, you know, but I digress... how can I help you?"

"Well, I know you're well into the USAAF 8th Air Force Fighter Command and if I recollect correctly you have had a couple of books published on the subject."

"Very true, what would you like me to do?"

"Well, I have this photograph that used to belong to an old family member. It's of a USAAF pilot kneeling on the wing of a P-51D with a large black Labrador, and I would really like to know his name, the pilot that is, not the dog, of course. On the back it is marked, *The Army Film and Photographic Unit (AFPU)."*

"Well, that should be easy enough. If it's AFPU, it will be official and more than likely catalogued. Just bring it round in the morning and I will see what I can do. I'm not scheduled to fly for a week, so it will be no hassle, give me an excuse to have a day off from decorating our daughter's bedroom. You know where I live, we haven't moved. It's the place where we used to hold the club meetings."

"Sure, I remember. It's not too far from me so… see you about ten then."

*

The next morning brought Kirsten to Roger Deacon's front door, where she was ushered into a large kitchen and given a cup of coffee by his wife, Penny. "Roger is out with the dog at the moment, should be back any minute. I understand you would like some help in identifying a World War Two pilot in an old photograph. He'll absolutely love doing that."

"Exactly, Penny, thing is, an anomaly has come up in my family tree and I'm trying to sort it out, quite complicated really."

"Oh, no need to explain, I know what families can be like… but as I said, he will love a bit of detective work like this. You won't believe the amount of reference books he's collected. You can hardly move in his office."

A loud crash as the back door opened, announced the arrival of the family Labrador, who had already figured out there was someone different in the house. Although he had never seen her before, he homed in on Kirsten, his swinging tail causing untold destruction to a waste bin and the vegetable rack. "Fine guard dog you are, and what have you done with your master?"

His master was right behind him. "Hello, Kirsten, been waiting long?"

"Five minutes, that's all. Penny has been looking after me."

They sat drinking coffee for ten minutes discussing their latest news, before Roger asked to see the photograph. "Might need my specs for this, the old short-range vision is not what it used to be!" He picked up the photograph, studied it for a few minutes and then turned it over. "Well, it's absolutely genuine, looks like one of the AFPU's original prints. Tell you what, leave it with me and I'll see what I can find out… I'm thinking we could discover a lot more than the pilot's name. There is an awful lot of detail here."

Kirsten's interest was immediately raised. "How do you mean?"

"Well, apart from the obvious, like the pilot and the stupid dog, who bears a real resemblance to this daft mutt," he pointed at the Labrador, "you can see suggestions of a row of small swastika kill markings under the canopy edge and part of the last letter of the aircraft's name, plus some chequered group nose markings. It's black and white, of course, but the cheques should narrow the fighter group down to just a few. My guess is that this is one of a professional set taken by the AFPU to celebrate something special like… possibly reaching ace status!"

"That's five victory kills, right?"

"Certainly is, as I said, leave it with me for the rest of the day and I'll give you a call tonight."

"Well, that's fantastic. Thank you so much, Roger."

Roger's wife was quick with a reply. "Well, that's the last I'll see of him for today, until he either gets hungry or thirsty, that is."

Kirsten apologised. "I'm so sorry, had you other things planned for today?"

"Well, he had mentioned he would make a start on decorating our daughter's bedroom but that can wait."

"Oh dear, please forgive me, Penny. Once this is all sorted, I'll treat you both to dinner, that's a promise. I can introduce you to a friend of mine who is over from the States. In fact, Roger may already know him. He's flying at the show this weekend," but Roger only had a vague recollection of the name Ven Carlson. Eager to start his investigations, he disappeared into his office. Kirsten thanked them both, said her goodbyes and left.

*

Ven's meeting with the Mustang owner and the general briefing with the show director all went according to plan, and he was about to call for a cab to take him back to his hotel when one of the other Mustang pilots asked him if he would like a lift, as he was going back to Cambridge in about half an hour; an offer he gladly accepted. He spent the intervening thirty minutes in the airfield museum bookshop, where he purchased one of Roger Deacon's books on the 8th Air Force Fighter Command.

On entering the hotel, the receptionist called him over and asked if he needed a table for dinner and, "Oh, your hire car has been delivered and here are the keys." Ven booked a table for eight and made his way up to his room, looking forward to a relaxing soak in the tub. As he climbed the stairs, he found himself saying, "Kirsten being Kirsten... as soon as I put one foot in the tub, the damned phone will go." He put one foot in the tub and the phone went.

*

Kirsten was sat on her couch with an open flight bag at her feet and surrounded by a pile of manuals when Roger Deacon called. Glancing at her watch, it was six o'clock.

"Hello, Roger, you're a man of your word. Did you have any joy with that photograph?"

"Well, yes and no really. Finding out his identity was easy, but being the smart ass I am, I did a bit of digging and that's where the trouble started."

"Trouble, what do you mean trouble?"

"Trouble is too strong a word maybe. Anomalies is a better way of putting it."

"OK, what sort of anomalies?"

"You know, Kirsten, this is really difficult to explain over the phone. Look, is there any chance you could pop round tomorrow? It would be so much easier, and I can show you what I've found."

"Sounds interesting, hope it's not bad news."

"No, nothing like that. I'm in all day, so just turn up when you can."

"I'm really intrigued. Is it OK if I bring Ven?"

"Of course you can... So see you when I see you."

*

Ven picked up the hotel room phone and, yes, it was Kirsten. She enquired how his day had gone and what he thought of the P-51 he was going to fly. "It's a real stunner, not long out of rebuild. The owner is very co-operative, must have spent a load of money putting it back in her 78th FG colours. The show director has everything organised to the last minute detail, so it should all go like a smoothly oiled machine. To be honest, I'm just so looking forward to getting back in the air again."

"I know the feeling. It'll be awhile for me but I'm definitely getting there... Ven, I'm calling in on Roger Deacon tomorrow. He wants to talk to me about that photograph. He's done a bit of research and he has a few things he wants to discuss. Fancy coming along with me? He doesn't live far from you."

"Sure, what time?"

"Well, I thought if we called in on him at about eleven o'clock, we could have lunch afterwards in Cambridge."

"OK, it's a deal but on one condition and that is... lunch is on me this time."

Kirsten laughed and reluctantly agreed. "I'll pick you up at ten thirty."

*

The following morning, Kirsten picked up Ven from his hotel and within fifteen minutes they were at Roger's house, where Penny and the dog greeted them. Penny was giving Ven the once-over. "So this is the mysterious Mr Carlson. Now you have introduced him to me, does this mean that dinner is off? No, please, I'm only joking!" Ven laughed; he'd never been called mysterious before. "Roger is in his office. Just go on in."

They were welcomed by Roger, who had not only the original photograph but also several others laid out on his desk. "Well, as I said, the first part of the puzzle was easy, as this is a catalogued official photograph."

Kirsten was eager. "So, Roger, don't keep us in suspense any longer. Who is it?" Roger passed her a piece of A5 paper which stated:

Captain Domenico D'Angelino 5 (7) kill fighter ace
326 Fighter Squadron
349th Fighter Group
USAAF Linton Grange, August 1944

Underneath, Roger had written:

From this photograph alone you cannot identify the aircraft, but the 349th FG purple and white nose checks and the last letter L of its name are clear enough. Could be Hell or Bell or many other things.

Kirsten studied it for a while. "Well, this seems quite straightforward, but why does it say 5 (7)?"

Roger agreed but continued. "Ah, this is where it starts getting complicated. He is credited with another two victories before the end of August, but then there is no more mention of him in the squadron records."

"So what happened to him?"

"Well, he is not listed as KIA (killed in action), WIA (wounded in action) or returned to the States after tour completion. I thought I had got the answer when I found him listed as killed in a ground accident!"

"What was the accident?"

"Even stranger. Although it was at Linton Grange, it was a B-26 Marauder take-off accident in August 1944."

Ven chipped in: "The infamous Widow Maker didn't fly well on one engine and no chance if it happened on take-off."

Kirsten was confused. "Why was he involved with Marauders?"

"Beats me. Maybe a visiting aircraft."

Ven nodded but added, "It's a strange one but not unknown, could have been a weather or Tech diversion. What else have you got?"

Roger passed them a print of four relaxed-looking pilots holding their flying helmets in their hands, stood in front of a Mustang. Ven, who held the print for a split second, showed visible signs of shock but controlled himself and said nothing. Kirsten asked if there was a problem but he just shook his head, remained silent and handed her the print. Kirsten took only a quick first glance at the four pilots but then did a double take. She stared in disbelief; her slightly delayed reaction then mirrored that of Ven. Roger couldn't understand. "What's up with you two? It's only an old World War Two image of four pilots. Can you see something which has eluded me?"

Kirsten and Ven turned, glanced at each other and then turned back to Roger. "No, please carry on."

Roger took back the print. "Well, apparently this is Red Flight, 326 Squadron, early August 1944. The four pilots are Red One – Captain Domenico D'Angelino, the guy in your picture, of course; Red Two – 2nd Lieutenant M.H.

Pepperman; Red Three – Lieutenant Victor Gilburtson and Red Four – Lieutenant Dave Zetterval. By the way, there was a reason for your surprise, wasn't there?"

"Oh, it was just seeing the whole of the guy's face in my photograph for the first time," Kirsten lied, but continued, "but I still don't see those anomalies you mentioned on the phone."

Roger picked up one of the other prints. "Well, how about this then?" Again, it was the same four pilots, stood in front of a Mustang aircraft, but the background was different, being the rear fuselage Star and Bar national insignia along with a large portion of the vertical tail. This time, however, only three of them were in their flying gear. The fourth, Pepperman, was in his full dress uniform. "Now look at the date. It's late September 1944, just before the 326th FG departed for France, and by that time Captain Domenico D'Angelino... had been dead for a month!"

Silence filled the room for a few seconds before Ven interjected. "Could be just a date error."

Roger agreed. "But here is another, take a look at this." He produced an excellent 326 squadron photograph, labelled *Air Field A-38 Montreuil, Northern France, December 1944*. The pin-sharp photograph showed three rows of pilots in dress uniform stood and seated on trestles with their names listed underneath. "Now, look at the guy extreme left, top row, recognise him?"

Kirsten and Ven both nodded. "Looks like Captain D'Angelino again."

"Right, now look at the names caption list."

"It says unknown."

"And he's the only one out of twenty-five plus pilots to be labelled thus. I have other similar photographs, but can you see where this is going?"

"Can this be logically explained in any way?"

"None that I can see."

"Well, at least I know who he was. By the way, are any of the four still alive?"

"Well, we know about D'Angelino. Dave Zetterval passed away in 2004 and Vic Gilburtson died in a flying training accident in the sixties. I've got nothing on Pepperman. He appears to have been wounded and placed on ground duties... disappeared into the system, if you like. So as they say, there the trail goes cold."

Ven asked if he could have another look at that third photograph again, the one where you can see the tail number of the P-51D, and... by the way, had he checked out the history of that aircraft? Roger was quite happy to answer that question. He had indeed, and this particular aeroplane had a very interesting history in that she had spent time with the famous 352nd FG at Bodney but in August 1944 had been battle-damaged, repaired and reissued to the 349th FG. Ven was looking very pensive again but Kirsten took control of the situation.

"Well, Roger, thank you so much for all your hard work, and you must believe me, I will be contacting Penny soon to set up that dinner I promised you."

Roger smiled and shrugged his shoulders. "Only sorry I couldn't bring things to a neat conclusion... thoroughly enjoyed myself doing it, though."

*

Kirsten and Ven sat silent in the BMW, parked 2 miles up the road in a lay-by. She turned to him. "What do you make of all that then?"

"I think you should go first, ladies first, remember."

"OK, here it is, you can believe this or not." She hesitated before going on. "Captain Domenico D'Angelino is more than a dead ringer for the guy I saw at the funeral."

Ven laughed. "I can top that. Captain Domenico D'Angelino is the guy who came up and spoke to me in the pub on Monday, and that aeroplane you can see in the photograph I double checked, well, would you believe this… it has the same tail number as… the *Guardian Angel*."

"Of course, the letter L. Good grief, no wonder we both looked so shocked. We must both be going nuts!"

Ven could not control his nervous laughter. "I must be nuts to hang around with you. I'm supposed to be relaxing on a flying holiday. I've only been here a few days and I feel I'm getting close to a breakdown."

Kirsten was now laughing too. "At least we can still laugh, but I tell you what, I will get to the bottom of this. Mike the Mint promised us an explanation tomorrow and I will get it out of him."

Ven made a comment about tough talk but then sat up, slapping his forehead. "Of course… that's it."

"What is?"

"Mike the Mint, don't you see it? The age, everything, it all fits!"

TWELVE

FIELDS OF GOLD

Kirsten and Ven sat in the courtyard of the Eagle pub in Cambridge enjoying a fish and chips lunch. "Well, what do you think of it?"

Ven leaned back, lifted his glass of lager and took a sip. "Think of what?"

"You know, sometimes you can be so bloody awkward. The fish and chips, of course."

"Language, please. I didn't think English ladies swore." He hesitated and then continued... "Sorry, I couldn't resist it. Well, to be perfectly honest, on a hot summer's day with a glass of cool beer and a beautiful English woman on the other side of the table, I... don't think it can be beat."

"Don't you suck up to me, Ven Carlson."

He laughed and decided to change the subject. "This city must have some real history. Do you know Cambridge well?"

"Well, I spent three years here at Cambridge doing my

engineering degree, and it's also where the local university air squadron gave me a taste for flying. But the call of the military wasn't strong enough, so, instead, I jumped at an airline flying scholarship when it was offered. The last few years have seen me visiting Aunt Kathryn quite regularly and her hospital was close, so all in all, yes, I know it quite well."

"So this pub is one of your old haunts."

She looked around before going on. "This pub has quite a place in history really, actually, two places in history."

Ven looked amused. "Two places? Please go on."

Kirsten put her head on one side, rested her chin on her fist and then continued.

"As you can imagine, with so many students and so much alcohol being consumed, each college tended to have its own watering hole. Back in the fifties, this place was very popular with researchers who worked at the Cavendish laboratory, and it was in this pub that Francis Crick and James Watson announced one day, to some lunchtime patrons, that they had discovered the secret of life."

"What did they mean, the secret of life?"

"Yea, strange thing to say, sounds like something from a science-fiction book, but it was just a little something about the double helix and the structure of DNA."

"Wow, you've got to be joking, in this very building? That's amazing. I feel privileged, but... you did say two, what else has it got to offer?"

"Well, there is another bar at the back, but if I take you in there I'll never get you out."

"That's it then, let's go."

Kirsten smiled and told him she just knew that would be his reaction but would like a cup of coffee first.

In the RAF bar, Ven was absolutely transfixed and couldn't believe that all the graffiti writing on the smoky brown ceiling had been put there sixty years ago by allied airmen, mostly RAF and Americans. "What did they use to write with?"

"The barman will probably give you a more accurate answer than I can, but I believe they used to stand on the tables and use cigarette lighters or candles to write their names and squadron numbers on the ceiling."

"Fantastic. It almost seems to talk to you. I wonder if the 326th is up there."

"Probably, but it might take all afternoon to find it."

Ven explained that someone must have taken the time, checked out every name and number up there, and made a key, so he walked over to the barman to ask but before he could start the conversation, the barman had produced two plastic laminated sheets with all the information on it. "Saw you looking, sir, and guessed you would be looking for these."

Ven scanned down the list and there it was: 326th Fighter Squadron, Linton Grange, 3 feet to the right of the ceiling rose light fitting. He thanked the barman and went back to Kirsten. "Well, according to the listing it should be... and, well, I'll be damned, there it is. What a small world we live in, Kirsten."

Ven settled the bill and Kirsten offered to show him some of the tourist spots. "That would be great but what I would really like is for you to show me some of the places that have special memories for you." Kirsten walked him about the city, pointing out things that were still the same from ten years before and others that had changed. As they walked, Ven asked if she had realised that she still referred to her grandmother as her Great-Aunt Kathryn, to which she replied, "No, not really, the discoveries of the last few days are still sinking in."

They ended up seated on the grass by the river. "You know, Kirsten, sitting here, I've realised I've wasted far too much of my life thrashing about the sky in old aeroplanes. There are so many other things to enjoy."

Kirsten agreed. "Me too, only difference is, I thrash about the sky in new aeroplanes."

Ven gave a chuckle. "Problem is, though, it's the only thing we both do well. Me, I have always put the *Angel* first, ruined any chance I've ever had of a long-term relationship. You won't believe this but apparently girls would prefer to talk about condos and drapes rather than fuel injection systems."

She laughed again. "No, really, I do find that hard to believe." She hesitated but then went on. "I was in a long-term relationship once but he was another pilot. I was based in Luton and he in Rome. We hardly saw anything of each other and both of us finally came to the conclusion it wasn't working. Basically, we both put our careers first."

Ven was thoughtful. "But is it possible to have both?"

"Guess so, look at Penny and Roger, happily married for twenty years. She was a senior flight attendant for the first ten years of their marriage whilst he was route flying, brought up two kids as well... Hey, this conversation is getting far too profound."

They sat, quietly thinking, mulling over the day's events. After a long silence, Ven was the first to speak. "Kirsten, I'm going to need your help to get through this. My whole approach to life is pragmatic. I find it very difficult to cope with things

I don't understand, and what with my encounter with that mystery guy in the pub on Monday and what Roger showed us today, well, it surpasses all my understanding. Yea, I know you can write it off, with various explanations, like coincidence and errors, but what are the chances of the aeroplane in that photo being the *Guardian Angel*? They built over 8,000 of them for God's sake. And to be honest, we both seem to be quietly blinding ourselves to what's happening, letting it all drift past us… quietly ignoring the giant elephant in the room if you like."

Ven expected a rebuke from Kirsten. In many ways, when faced with life's troubles, she was much stronger than him, but she surprised him by turning to him with what she couldn't hide: a tear in her eye. She whipped away from him and wiped it dry with her wrist. "This is your captain crying… What do you make of that, Ven Carlson? Maybe it's me who needs the help."

Ven put his arm around her but for a time didn't know what to say. "Hey, we're a team, we just have to be open and honest about it, manage it if you like. Both of us are so deep into this, we can't give up now."

Kirsten was so mad that she had shown her emotions in front of him. "You know, you are right. I feel I am much closer to sorting out for ever the mysteries of my mother's side of the family, and knowing the lady I called Great-Aunt Kathryn for most of my life was really my Grandmother Rose, well, that was a fantastic revelation. It could be that part of what you saw just now was a release of joy. On the other hand, if only I had known earlier, I could have done so much more for her."

Ven was quick to answer. "But you didn't know, did you, Kirsten? So don't torture yourself. There is no need." She relaxed a little. Although she obviously knew the answer, she enquired, "So what is this large pachyderm that needs talking about?"

"Well, do either of us have an explanation for this mystery man who keeps appearing?"

"Oh, come on, Ven, say it. We both know what you're trying to say... the bloody ghost."

A shiver ran down his spine. "I was trying to avoid that word but OK, for starters, what's your opinion on the 'G' word?"

"Ask me that question a few months ago, before all this started, and I would have given you short shrift, but when you have been on the receiving end, it kind of shapes your opinion somewhat. I suppose the standard cop-out answer would be, 'I have an open mind,' but that's weak and, in fact, I have given the subject some thought recently. In simplistic terms, this place we are in right now, for instance, I mean Cambridge, it's full of researchers of all shapes and forms. In fact, there are more researchers here than there ever has been. What do researchers do? They try to find out, using scientific reasoning, the answers to things we do not know and understand. Maybe the 'G' word, as you call it, fits neatly into the 'what we don't have an answer for' category."

Ven was impressed. "You know, I can't argue with that, so, for the time being at least, I will do what I always do."

"And what's that?"

"Put my worries in an imaginary box and keep a tight lid on it."

"Exactly, and who knows, maybe everybody has a box with a secret in it, just like my grandmother!" Ven was happier now; a problem shared was a problem halved. "Well, I ought

to be getting you back. Early start tomorrow, remember."
Ven sensed Kirsten had taken this conversation as far as she
wanted to for the time being.

"Whatever you say. You're in charge. By the way, did I
tell you I have a set of wheels now? To save you a few miles,
I'll meet you at the churchyard car park and we can go up to
the airfield in one vehicle, say… meet at three thirty." Kirsten
agreed and they set off for the Lion Yard, where they had
parked her car.

*

In the flat, the message light was flashing on her answerphone.
She clicked the answer button and it was the vicar of St Mary's.
"Please call me when you have a spare minute. Something
very sad has happened." She made herself a sandwich and a
cup of coffee and sat reflecting. She had been doing a lot of
reflecting lately. When and where was all this going to end?

She called the vicar, who seemed genuinely upset, and
enquired as to what had happened.

"Well, late this afternoon, I returned from my weekly
visiting rota, stood in the churchyard thinking how beautiful
and tidy it all looked in the summer sunshine and how
lucky I was to have a handyman like Mike, when I noticed
someone sitting on the memorial seat bench under the yew
tree. Realising it was Mike, I thought I would go and have
a word with him. As I approached, I perceived that he was
sleeping. An excellent job well done and at his age why not
have a nap? I thought. His old Raleigh bicycle was propped
up at the far end of the seat and all his tools had been cleaned
and were placed neatly in a pile by his side. He looked so at

peace with the world. I gave a small cough to try and wake him but there was no response, so I reached out and gently shook his shoulder, but to my horror, he slowly keeled over. I called an ambulance, of course, but they told me he must have been dead for over an hour and in all likelihood there probably would have been nothing I could have done, even if I had been there!"

"I'm so sorry to hear that. Presumably, the ambulance took him away?"

"Yes indeed, and I will do all I can to make sure he gets a decent burial. I have already contacted the farmer up at the airfield, who has promised to help, and he will go over tomorrow and sort out Mike's few meagre possessions, which of course can't be many. Anyway, it means maybe we will never solve the mystery of your aunt's funeral."

"Please don't concern yourself too much over that, Reverend, and anyway, I am making good progress using other lines of enquiry." Kirsten stopped and considered what was happening to her. Was she now using similar language to her father? But she made one more request. "This may sound a little strange, Reverend, but when it comes to his funeral, please let me know. I would very much like to attend." The vicar agreed and she thanked him for all his help.

Now she had a problem, in fact, two problems. Was it indeed worthwhile going at all tomorrow and, if so, should she tell Ven? Something was telling her she had to go, and she would not tell Ven until they met at the churchyard car park in the morning.

*

The two bleary-eyed airfield investigators reached the churchyard car park almost at the same time. "Hi, Ven, forgot to remind you to bring a flashlight, hope you've remembered!"

"Sure have, look at this beauty. The receptionist at the hotel hooked it out for me, even got a spare battery set."

"Getting chummy with the receptionist, are we?" She paused but then continued. "Maybe we should take my car, as these roads can be quite narrow and... I don't know if you noticed but patches of mist are beginning to form and it's quite possible it could turn into fog and clamp right down up there."

Ven nodded his agreement; what she had suggested seemed eminently sensible. He parked his car well off the road and got into the BMW. She turned towards him and made her confession. "Ven... there is something I have to tell you... Mike the Mint... will not be there!"

Ven's face was the epitome of confusion. "So why in hell are we still going? I hope he has got a good excuse."

"None better."

"Oh yea and what's that?"

"He's dead!"

"Well, I guess we can excuse him for that. What on earth happened?" Kirsten explained the vicar's phone call and apologised for not giving him a choice about this morning.

"Well, we're here now, so I guess we had better do it!" She thanked him for his understanding and set off for Linton Grange.

On the way, Ven made his own confession. "Kirsten... you know you once asked me what happened that day in Arizona and I danced all around an answer, saying something got you out of that near-fatal spin. Well, I should have said that something or someone got you out of that spin."

It was Kirsten's turn to look confused. "I don't understand. How could it have been someone?"

Ven took a deep breath. "Well, Rusty… God bless him… swears on his grandmother's life that when the *Guardian Angel* came over the fence that day, there was a…" He waited and took another deep breath before going on. "There was a second person in the rear seat."

Kirsten nearly ran off the road but regained control and pulled over. "That's complete and utter nuts… he had obviously been drinking!"

"You know, that was exactly my first reaction, but I have talked to the club barman and he reckons, to the best of his recollection, Rusty may have had a few but he was definitely not drunk when he set off in the truck. And you know what – and I bet you never thought you would hear me say this – there is a part of me that believes him. There… I've said it."

Kirsten reacted coolly, restarted the car and continued the short journey before turning to Ven. "You know what, Ven Carlson, after what you just said, we are definitely going through with this."

Ven said nothing and just sat in silence. As they got closer, her prophecy of fog looked more and more likely and so by the time they reached the concreted area where they parked, you could hardly see 5 feet in front of you. Ven was unsettled. "Kirsten, you know, thinking about this now, it's utter madness. We could get lost on this old airfield and spend half the day up here trying to find our way back to the car."

"Please, Ven, don't let me down now. We must try. All we

have to do is find the old iron plough and turn left and we are there."

He hesitated but then stepped out of the car. "OK... let's go then, flashlights at the ready." They had hardly gone 10 yards when he froze. "What the hell is that? I saw something moving, did you?"

"No, not really, it's the fog. It plays tricks with your eyes and brain." He stopped and pointed. "There it is again, don't say you didn't see it that time?"

"I did, it's a four-legged animal, could be a fox."

"No, no, wait a minute, it's old Laddie the Collie. He's guiding us again through the fog."

Ven was searching the track margins for the plough, but judging distances in the fog was nigh on impossible. In the end, they did not have to worry, as the dog, who knew exactly where he was, stopped when he came to the turning and led them off towards the old domestic area. Once they were safely on track, the old dog turned, barked and disappeared into the darkness. They walked quickly along the track, looking for the bend that led to the domestic site and Mike's hut. Ven slowed down and pulled Kirsten back. "Have you noticed something different about the track? All the tumbleweed has gone and the surface feels much smoother."

Kirsten had to agree and then made an observation of her own. "Is it my imagination or can I hear vehicle engine noise?"

Ven swung round. "It's not your imagination, there is a vehicle coming up behind us with what looks like hooded headlights."

Within seconds, the Jeep was upon them, a loud curse

of, "Out of the way, paddle-feet," was heard as it sped by and disappeared into the thick fog.

Ven had an explanation: "Of course, it has to be the re-enactors, still going through with their practice."

"Well, they could have been a little more consid—" She did not have time to complete the sentence before a second vehicle was on them, a fire truck accompanied by more oaths, not so pleasant this time. "Looks like we are in their way, better keep to the side of the track." This was a good move, as the next assailant was an old RAF model fuel bowser, which needed every inch of the track.

Ven was worried. "You know, I don't remember seeing a fire truck or a fuel bowser in their inventory when they were parked outside the pub." Kirsten had no answer. They reached the bend and within a few minutes were on the edge of the domestic area, which felt and looked very different. For a start, there was no smell of pigs, and dim lights could be seen in many of the hut windows, which now appeared to be fully glazed.

Kirsten pulled Ven closer. "This isn't computing. Something is definitely not right here."

"Well, we can't make a run for it. We'd just end up getting hopelessly lost."

"Just keep going. Look, there is the turning that leads down to Mike's hut. It's only about 20 yards down there," and sure enough, there was the hut, but again there was something different about it. Ven realised what it was: there was definitely no white flagpole the last time they were there.

They stood in front of the hut which, although surrounded by the noise of voices and running motors, was shrouded in darkness, trying to figure out what to do next. Kirsten had the answer. "Well, we have an invitation, don't we? Let's go on in."

Ven stepped forward and tried one of the front double doors; it was unlocked. Gingerly, he opened it and stepped inside, closely followed by Kirsten, both making full use of their flashlights. "Well, I'll be damned. This is just like stepping back in time."

Inside, there were four beds, each with a side locker and wardrobe. Areas of the curved walls were covered in WW2 pin-ups. On top of the small pot-bellied stove was a brown envelope addressed to *Miss Kirsten Davies,* which Ven picked up and handed to its intended recipient. Kirsten took the envelope and waved it gently from side to side in front of her face. "Impressive, but nevertheless a bit of an anti-climax, though. Don't know what I was expecting really!"

Kirsten's disappointment was short-lived as the ceiling lamps started to flicker on and off and then, with an almighty crash, both rear doors to the hut swung open. Four shimmering images stood before them and saluted. All four were dressed in full flying kit, obviously ready for a mission. Kirsten and Ven were rooted to the spot, although some automated response in Ven made him blurt out, "Is it the four horsemen of the apocalypse or the four musketeers?"

The image on the extreme left, Gilburtson, laughed. "I like that, and just the kind of thing I would say."

Dom D'Angelino raised his hand and quietly stepped forward. The blood in Kirsten's veins ran cold; her reserves of courage were almost completely burnt up. "Do not be afraid, Kirsten. All we want of you is that you should know the whole truth, so that the story of your grandmother and the woman she was will not be lost."

He stepped back just as a voice outside shouted, "Red Flight transport, move yourselves. Engine start in fifteen minutes." The four figures saluted once more, slowly turned and disappeared into the darkness.

Ven was suddenly released from his self-inflicted paralysis. "What in hell was that? Nobody is ever going to believe this, I don't believe it."

Kirsten, who could not remember if she had been breathing for the last minute, pulled herself together. "I don't think it was intended for anyone else… it was just for us."

Ven was staring at the doors. "Who closed the doors?"

Kirsten did not bother to answer. She just took his arm and pulled him towards the front door. "Let's get out of here, something big is going on outside."

They stood by the flagpole in foggy darkness, surrounded by all the activity of an early-morning mission. Ven swore he could hear the sound of Wright R-1820 Cyclone engines droning overhead. "Listen, that will be the B-17s already on their way." On the other side of the little street, the door of another hut swung open and an airman emerged with a parachute slung over his shoulder. He made a curious clinking sound as he slowly trudged along the concrete, making his way towards the old control tower. He paused and gave a friendly wave. They both automatically raised their hands in acknowledgement but then froze… he had no face. Ven glanced at Kirsten and then back to where the man had been standing, but he was gone. "I didn't like that one little bit."

"Me neither." The only thing she could think to add was, "Should be getting light soon."

At that moment, the familiar sound of a Packard Merlin 1650 bursting into life could be heard, followed by a whole cacophony chorus of tens of others doing the same thing. There was no need to talk; they both knew what was happening. The Mustangs were now beginning to move out, ready for take-off. In his head, Ven was going through all the motions the pilots in those fighter planes were going through, the motions he knew so well; he was pensive. "It must be clearer out there… no way you can take off in this."

Kirsten had started to relax. "Wouldn't surprise me at all, fog can be so localised at this time of the year in this part of the country."

The noise was now a constant throb as the 349th Fighter Group waited for take-off clearance. Did he imagine a green glow in the sky over towards the main runway or was it real? He had just got out the words, "There's the Green," when the engine noise rose to a crescendo. The Mustangs were taking off in pairs on alternate runways. He counted them as pair after pair accelerated down the runway. When he got to twenty-four, he stopped. "That's full group strength, forty-eight machines," but he was wrong. One more pair followed and the noise ceased.

Kirsten had the answer. "That'll be the two spares. You see… I do know a little."

Ven was happier now; they both seemed to realise that whatever had happened was over, and they turned and started walking back the way they had come. Above their heads, the mist was getting thinner. In the east, a hazy sun was breaking through; morning came up in a pale reverse fade. Ven pointed at the old dilapidated huts. "Look, they're back to normal, busted roofs and windows."

Kirsten had now completely regained her composure. "And you can certainly smell the porkers!"

By the time they reached the main track, the sun was displaying a glorious cerise sunrise, causing the surrounding cornfields to glisten as the morning dew reflected its rays. After a significant period of contemplative silence, Kirsten was the first to speak again. "I don't know why, but the part of me that's saying I should be a quivering traumatised wreck isn't working. I just have this overriding feeling of total peace and closure. Do you feel the same, Ven?"

Ven's face creased in a smile, for the first time in over an hour. "Know what, you've taken the words right out of my mouth. I could not have put it better. I will certainly never forget what has happened here this morning and definitely won't be putting this in the box." She turned, looped her arm through his and, with no more words needed, they walked steadily back to the car.

They sat in the car, both staring straight ahead. "Have you still got your letter?"

"I have, but feel I need somewhere quiet to read it. Could contain a few more surprises." She started the car and drove off back along the narrow road that led back to the village and church, but before they had gone a mile, she pulled over and parked by a farm track which stretched out up a slight incline, dissecting two fields of ripe golden barley.

Ven understood. "I guess it's time for your letter." Kirsten slipped a finger through the envelope flap, opened it and pulled out a handwritten letter which she proceeded to read aloud.

Dear Miss Davies,

If all has gone according to plan, you will be reading this at about 05:30 on Thursday morning. As you can imagine, living the life I have over the last fifty years, I have neither written nor received many letters, so please excuse any errors as I am a little out of practice.

The first thing to point out is I am not the inspiration for this letter. That is entirely down to Captain Domenico D'Angelino, who was determined that on our leaving, you should be fully cognisant of the events that have shaped your life. He is also well aware that a young woman of your undoubted intelligence and determination will have worked many things out for herself. However, his intent is that what you have seen and witnessed this morning will fill in any gaps.

My part of the story is small, as I am the junior member of the team that called itself Red Flight 326 Squadron, 349th Fighter Group USAAF. Although the young men of America only inhabited this East Anglian air base for two years, they left an indelible mark on the surrounding countryside and its people, who took them to their hearts. Domenico D'Angelino was an outstanding leader and a superb human being in every respect. He not only saved my life on more than one occasion but he taught me how to do the job I had been sent here to do. However, none of us are without our failings and both of us made mistakes, he through his unflinching bravery trying to save a friend, an act which cost him his life and sentenced his beloved girl, Rose, to a lifetime of nightmarish torment. My own mistake was much simpler, as I selfishly did not walk away from the love of a married woman when providence dictated that I should, but this is not about me.

You may not be aware but he has been watching over you since you were born. His one deep regret is that he was not able to save your mother on that tragic fateful night, *but things were different that day in Arizona when fate turned on you, a spare seat and a set of dual controls in the aeroplane he loved. What could be better? (He has asked me to address a note to Mr Carlson… she still drops a port wing a split second before the stall, which made getting out of that spin real tricky… please get it fixed.)*

With the passing of your grandmother, I was the last piece in the puzzle and so, after my removal from this mortal coil, it was decided, as kindred spirits, that we should go out in style, on one last mission. Do not be afraid. All over East Anglia you will find old air bases with similar stories to tell as our own. The spirits are simply waiting for the right moment to depart, they will not hurt you. We ask but just one thing and that is that the young men of the 8th Air Force should not be forgotten. They suffered heavily, with one in four of Fighter Command pilots never going home and the 8th in general losing over 26,000 young American men in the three years they were here. If we can leave just one final important message, it will be this. I do not know the author but it fits beautifully:

Do not forget the defenders of your country
If you forget them then you forget your country

Yours faithfully,
MH Pepperman

Ven was the first to speak. "That's really rich. If the perfect captain and his friends had not got the port main-plane shot full of 20mm cannon shell holes, it would not have the small aerodynamic idiosyncrasy it has today."

Kirsten smiled and slowly shook her head. "You do realise that you're trying to pick an argument with someone who has been dead sixty years, don't you?"

Ven clenched his teeth. "OK, point taken."

They both leaned back, enjoying the warming sun which was now starting to fill the eastern horizon of the big East Anglian sky. Ven turned and looked to the south, where the sound of an approaching aircraft could be heard. "I would recognise that beautiful engine prop combination noise anywhere. It's got to be a Mustang, but who in hell is up this early in the morning practising?" They both spotted it at the same time; it was coming their way at about 2,000 feet. Without thinking, they both stepped out of the car, watching the approaching aeroplane intently.

The nose of the Mustang gently dipped, picking up speed before smoothly pulling up into the vertical and continuing into a perfect loop. Ven's memory flashed back to that afternoon in Arizona when he first saw Kirsten performing aerobatics in the *Guardian Angel*. Every pilot had their own signature way of performing aerobatics, and the expert eye could often tell who was flying an aeroplane. The thought ran through his mind that whoever this was, his handling was so similar to Kirsten's. He decided to say nothing and just watch this expert at work, flying a Mustang with the same delicate skill a maestro would play a Stradivarius violin.

Kirsten broke the spell. "Beautiful flying, so smooth. Must be someone practising for Saturday. Do you recognise the aircraft?"

"Can't say I do." He hesitated. "Oh, come on... Look at the markings, purple and white nose checks."

Kirsten had spotted the markings as well. "349th Fighter Group… I think we both know who this is."

The Mustang made one more low last pass, waggled her wings and departed in the direction from which she had come. They both watched in silence as the aeroplane disappeared into the distance, the sun glinting on her polished wings. For a moment, they both stood there transfixed, but then Ven leaned over and whispered in her ear, "Kirsten, do you ever get the feeling that someone is watching you?"

"No, not often, but right now… Yes." They both turned slowly and not for the first time that morning were rooted to the spot. There, not 10 yards away, was a young USAAF captain and his English Rose. The couple slowly turned and walked hand in hand up the gentle incline of the farm track. Each side of their path was lined with waving rows of golden barley, over which summer swallows swooped and twisted. Neither Kirsten nor Ven felt the need to speak, and simply watched.

At the top of the track, Dom and Rose stopped, turned and waved for the last time, before slowly disappearing over the brow of the little hill. "Shall we go after them?"

"I don't know what good that would do, Kirsten, and there is no need. We both know exactly who that was."

Kirsten took his arm and pulled him to her side. "That… Ven Carlson… was my grandmother and grandfather… My *Guardian Angel* and his Rose, truly together at last."

They got back into the car and set off for the village. Kirsten was showing a remarkable level of composure after all that had happened to her in the last hour or so. "Anyway, you were asking about why we Brits drive on the left."

"I did!"

Kirsten had spotted the markings as well. "349th Fighter Group… I think we both know who this is."

"Well, think on this, most people are right- or left-handed?"

"Right-handed."

"So if you are riding your horse along this very country lane in the 18th century, on which side would you hang your sword?"

"I suppose on the left, and if I needed it, I would draw it across my body."

"Exactly. That way, you wouldn't get it caught up in the hedge, would you?"

"Ah, now I see, so Napoleon was left-handed?"

"That's it, I give up…!"

In the churchyard of St Mary's, the Reverend Brown was making himself busy. One of his self-confessed failings was his passion for order. He disliked disorder in any shape or form, and visitors who left unattended, dead or dying flowers on graves were the object of a strong dislike. The thought had occurred to him that the funeral of Kirsten's Great-Aunt Kathryn had been well over ten days ago and any flowers laid that day would be well past their best; he would go and check.

He made his way slowly towards the grave, wondering who he could call on to help keep the churchyard neat and tidy now that Mike was sadly no longer with us. His arrival at the grave provided a pleasant surprise; the flowers looked as fresh as the day they were placed there. His curiosity was drawn to the grave next door. An alteration had been made to the headstone engraving. This was not unusual. It could happen for many reasons, the most common being the addition to a double grave, such as a husband and wife. But this surely could not be the case; the Collins couple had been laid to rest thirty years ago. He knelt on both knees and peered at the inscription, which had been expertly altered. It now read:

IN LOVING MEMORY OF
JANE COLLINS 1901–1972
AND JACK COLLINS 1896–1962,
MOTHER AND FATHER OF TWO LOVING SONS,
WHO GAVE THEIR LIVES IN THE
1939–1945 CONFLICT,
AND THEIR LOVING DAUGHTER, ROSE

AUTHOR'S NOTES

The seed for this book was first planted in a pub. (I'm sure it's not the first time this has happened and it certainly won't be the last.) It had been a long day travelling back some distance by car and, although not far from our home in Newmarket, the attraction of a comforting pub meal and a little alcohol on a cold winter's night was just too great. My two travelling companions were my wife, Annette, and our daughter, Juliet. Sitting at the table next to a roaring log fire with three Irish whiskies, all three of us were in a somewhat relaxed frame of mind. The conversation turned to books we had recently read and those we had enjoyed the most. My contribution to the conversation was standout boring, as my reading was mainly reference-based, whilst my wife had a passion for crime and romantic novels and my daughter possessed a strong penchant for the paranormal. When it came to my turn to describe something that had intrigued me during my recent reading, I mentioned the fact that in many of the WW2 books I had read on the RAF and USAAF – that is in those that contained group photographs of aircrew – invariably in the name lists that were printed under those images, one of the names would be listed as *unknown*! How could this be? Someone had obviously carried out masses of research to find twenty-three names, but who was the twenty-fourth, and why was he invariably positioned at the left- or right-hand extremity of the back row? Unintentionally, I had really started something. My wife and daughter simultaneously had the answer, "A ghost," and so was born *Harvest of a Golden Sky*.

Although I had written several murder mystery plays for my local village theatre group, this was to be my first attempt at a novel, a task I found extremely daunting. As my whole life has been spent in aviation, with the last forty-five years in a technical training capacity, writing about aeroplanes came easy to me. My main worry was would my writing style be crushed by the concept principle I had used throughout my career? This was KISS, or, as most of us will know it, 'Keep It Simple, Stupid'. Early on, someone far brighter than me had written: *'Anyone can construct a complicated description of a simple device, but it takes real skill to deliver an accurate simple description of a complex device'*. Would my style be over-simplistic? I hope not but will leave it to the reader to decide!

The real hero of *Harvest of a Golden Sky* is, of course, the North American P-51 Mustang, the aeroplane that enabled the bombers of the 8th Air Force to fly accompanied and protected all the way into the deep reaches of the Third Reich and back. When Reichsmarschall Hermann Göring allegedly said, "*When I saw Mustangs over Berlin I knew the jig was up,*" I think he really meant it.

The P-51D version of the Mustang, with over 8,000 built, was the most popular with the USAAF 8th Air Force fighter pilots. The new teardrop bubble canopy, which rectified the limited rear visibility problems of earlier models, plus its superb long-range and extra pair of point fifty Browning machineguns, made it the machine the 8th Fighter Command desperately needed. Flying the P-51D, especially on long missions, was not always straightforward. The addition of the 85 US gal self-sealing fuel tank aft of the pilot's seat (which had been introduced in the P-51B) could seriously affect the aircraft's centre of gravity. When this tank was full, the centre of gravity of the Mustang was moved dangerously close to the aft limit. As a result of this, very careful fuel handling was required of the pilot, with only relatively gentle manoeuvres permitted until this tank was down to about 25 US gal and the external tanks had been dropped. As the Mustang pilots used to say, the internal wing tanks were only there to get you home. This was one of the very few vices the Mustang possessed and if handled correctly it was (until the advent of the jet Messerschmitt Me 262) more than a match for anything the Luftwaffe could put up against it.

Before leaving the military and technical aspects of the 8th Fighter Command, I feel it essential that mention must be made of the effort and logistics required in putting together the USAAF 8th Air Force Bomber Command offensive in England. Consider this; each B17 or B24 bomber usually carried a crew of ten, and bomber raids of 1,000 aeroplanes were quite common and a raid such as the 'Maximum Effort' of Christmas Eve 1944 could top 2,000. Along with the bombers, there would, of course, be the 500 to 1,000 protecting fighters. Simple mathematics comes up with the staggering figures that there could be 10,500 to 21,000 American young men in the air on any given day when such raids took place. In any other war scenario, a battle involving that amount of men would have been considered a major one. Yet, sadly, many of these almost daily huge conflicts have been forgotten. The cost in men and material was vast. At the beginning of the offensive, in 1942/43, before the introduction of fighters that could escort the bombers all the way to the target and back, mission losses were very high, on occasion even reaching twenty per cent. Such figures were obviously unsustainable. It was the advent of the long-range escort P-51 Mustang that enabled the whole thing to work. Nevertheless, in the three years or so that the 8th Air Force operated in Europe, it suffered more than 47,000 casualties, with more than 26,000 dead.

So what about the logistics? The construction of bases for the 8th Air Force, which included sixty-seven bomber bases (most of which were in East Anglia at a cost of about 100 million pounds each in today's money), was part of the largest civil engineering programme ever undertaken in the UK. Amazingly, some of these bases were constructed in a matter of months. Just before I leave the figures, think of this: each B17 would take 1,700 gallons of fuel, so a 2,000 bomber raid would need nearly three and a half million gallons of fuel, not to mention, at a bomb load of 4,000lbs per aeroplane, eight million lbs of bombs, this for one day's work. The mind truly boggles. Where did it all come from?

Today, only a few of the bases are recognisable, much of the runway concrete having been broken up and used in civil engineering projects like motorways. However, if you can find one that still exists, it's well worth a visit. Try visiting

Rougham Control Tower, for instance (but watch out for the local ghost).

The locations used in this book, as well as some of the units involved, are a mixture of actual and imaginary; Linton Grange, the 349th Fighter Group and the 326th Fighter Squadron are, of course, all imaginary, whilst Bodney and the 352nd FG are very real, their fame and achievements being legendary, as indeed the same could be said for any fighter group of the 8th. If I have accidently shown any individual or group of individuals in a bad light, it was certainly not intentional. I have the greatest respect for every one of the over 350,000 USAAF personnel who served and called East Anglia their home during WW2.

In a previous paragraph, I mentioned the Rougham Control Tower (Rougham Airfield AAF Station 468, Bury St Edmunds, Suffolk) as a place well worth a visit. A quick look at a photograph of the condition it was in before its restoration and comparing that to what it is now will show just how much the preservation group has achieved. I also mentioned that Rougham has a resident ghost. In fact, if you visit most deserted Second World War RAF or USAAF stations, invariably, you will find some local who has a ghostly tale or two to frighten you with. Why is this? Well, airfields are by their nature often flat, lonely, desolate places. Aeroplanes need lots of space, and any airfield will have a perimeter circumference of several miles.

There are two natural factors which can quite easily lift the scariness factor on an airfield. One is fog and the other is darkness. Personally, I have experienced both. As a nineteen-year-old RAF junior technician serving on 36 Squadron RAF Colerne near Bath – where rules were, I have to say, not always one hundred per cent obeyed – one night, I was ordered along with a senior aircraftsman (SAC) to take the Land Rover, run over to the ASF hangar and pick up a boost gauge from the stores counter. (The duty storeman had departed for his late supper, which he was perfectly entitled to do.) Whilst there, we had to pick up two sets of four-wheel oxygen charging trolleys. (These were supposed to be towed one at a time, as if you attempted to pull two at any more than 10MPH, they would decide to snake, with possible disastrous results.) What I have not explained was that it was eleven o'clock on a cold November evening with ten-tenths fog. My companion had a civilian driving licence but had only been on the squadron a week, being recently posted in. I only had a provisional, and that was for two wheels only. The plan according to '*Chiefy*' was that I knew where I was going but couldn't drive, but my companion could drive but didn't know where he was going. Together, we would do it.

Apparently, the fog had well and truly settled in and was not expected to clear until the following morning, so there was no activity on the base at all, or so they told us. Off we set with the keys to ASF (Aircraft Servicing Flight) and the oxygen bottle compound. (We didn't have to heft the bottles onto the trolleys; there would be two new trolleys waiting for us, making it a simple pick-up job.) We were not a happy team, complaining bitterly, "Why has half the shift been stood down, leaving us to frig about with oxygen bottles? Why couldn't the riggers do it?"

It is hard enough to find your way about featureless airfields in the dark, let alone the fog, there being no kerb edge to the taxiway and only the occasional light to guide you. Somehow, we safely reached the ASF hangar, which was in complete darkness. All we had was one of those green L-shaped service flashlights, which gave out as much light as a couple of cigarettes. We managed to open the hangar-side door and step inside. My companion spoke. "Where is the hangar lights, master switch?" to which I replied, "How the hell do I know? I only worked here on day shift for a couple of weeks." The stores counter was down the eastern end of the hangar; the task should be simple. At that moment, accompanied by a grinding squeak and crash, the side door swung closed.

"How did that happen? There is no wind, hope it's not a dead lock." My companion did not appear duly concerned and we set off in complete darkness for the end of the hangar. Halfway there, I tripped over a 2-inch-thick aircraft 28V DC power cable, the famed giant black rubber snake so much loved by aircraft fitters. I got up but my companion had disappeared. Above my head, the hangar roof was groaning and something high up was making a flapping noise. I just wanted to get out of there. Eventually, I found the store counter and a small box with a serviceable label marked 'Boost Gauge', which I grabbed and then made for the exit as fast as I could. Mysteriously, the door was now wide open again! I shouted for my companion but there was no reply. Thinking that he could look after himself, I made my way back to the Land Rover and, sure enough, there he was sitting inside; fat, dumb, warm and happy. All I could get out of him was a simple, "Sorry, I didn't feel safe in there."

We picked up the oxygen trolleys and against the rules decided to pull both trolleys at the same time so we would not have to come back again. To cut a long story short, it took us over an hour to get back to the 36 Squadron hangar, having got completely and utterly lost and ending up on the main runway, where one of the trolleys kindly decided to detach itself. During the recovery of the trolley, we both heard what I swear to this day was the sound of four Bristol Hercules engines belonging to a Handley Page Hastings on approach. Were we about to get crushed by 50,000lbs of Handley Page's finest? We did not wait to find out, coupling up the errant trolley in record time and getting off that runway very quickly. The fog can play real tricks with your ears (and mind).

I have one more personal tale of ghostly goings-on at an airfield. In 1943, United States Army Air Forces Station 169 Stansted Mountfitchet was home to the B-26 Marauders of the 344th Bomb Group 9th Air Force. Today, of course, we know it better as London Stansted Airport but for many years up until its modernisation, which started in the late eighties, it was very little used as a civil airport, its main use during the intervening years being that of a maintenance base with a company called Aviation Traders Engineering Ltd (ATEL), maintaining aircraft in two of the old hangars. The ATEL Training School, where I worked, was set well away from the two hangars on the opposite side of the airfield next to the fuel farm and small general aviation park. The school was built around a large old 9th Air Force Quonset hut with basically two wood and glass flat roof extensions. The central corridor had no windows, with the classroom entry doors on the right. At one end of the long corridor there was an instructors' common room, with washrooms located at the other end. Some thoughtful individual had put the corridor light switch at the far end so that in winter, if you were last to leave, you had to plunge yourself into complete darkness and then grope your way to the other end where the main door was located.

To earn a little extra, I volunteered to run an evening class for a group of engineers who wished to expand their licence coverage. The course started at six o'clock and finished at eight. This meant that on evening-class nights, the cleaning ladies could not start their cleaning until we had all left. The engineers, who had usually come straight from work, did not hang about when class finished and once we had tidied up, we were usually all away by eight fifteen. On arrival at work one winter's morning, I was invited into the training manager's office and asked, "What happened here last night?"

Totally bemused, I could only reply, "What did happen?" Apparently, the contents of every wastepaper bin in the school had been emptied out of the common-room window onto the flowerbeds below. It turned out that well after the students and I had departed the night before, the cleaning lady had starting cleaning one of the classrooms when she heard what she thought were American voices outside in the corridor, but when she looked, there was no one there. This happened every time she went into a classroom. Eventually, she got so scared that she just threw the bin contents out of the window and scarpered. Her supervisor found her, terrified, waiting outside under a street lamp. He then went back and locked up the school. The cleaning company had made a complaint to ATEL referencing students and/or the instructor playing tricks on their cleaner. After pointing out that we had all left by 8:15 pm, which was confirmed by the students, the cleaning company apologised, but the cleaners from that day on all refused to enter the school building during the hours of darkness unless they were accompanied!

Sadly, the last facet of *Harvest of a Golden Sky* which needs an explanation is, 'The Mental Deficiency Act of 1913'. This really was an Act of Parliament of the United Kingdom which made provisions for the institutional treatment of people deemed to be 'feeble-minded' and 'morally defective'. It was not effectively repealed until the introduction of the Mental Health Act of 1959. The original Act of 1913 allowed local authorities, when petitioned (typically) by parents, to certify and institutionalise unmarried pregnant women. At the time, mental defects were believed by some to be the cause of a woman's immorality. The numbers are unknown and probably few but, as an example, some sad victims were discovered in mental hospitals as late as 1971, having been there since the 1920s. My late father-in-law, who ran a care home until the late nineties and who by necessity and for obvious reasons closely co-operated with the local mental health authorities, once confided in me that the local mental hospitals still held several of these unfortunate women patients, now quite elderly, who could not be rehabilitated, as they had become totally and utterly institutionalised, having for the last fifty years known no other life than that of the hospital. So, in 2005, there may well have been ladies like Kirsten's Grandmother Rose still trapped in mental institutions whose only sin was something that today would not even raise an eyebrow.

Richard F. Sugg

GLOSSARY OF TERMS AND ABBREVIATIONS

Over the years, the world of military aviation has developed its own language; some official, some not. Here you will find some of the words, terms, abbreviations and technical expressions used in the story which may not be familiar to you. Hopefully, it may help.

Big Friends – US Fighter pilot slang for the B-17 and B-24 Bombers. (Bomber crews referred to the Fighters as 'Little Friends.')

B-26 Marauder – American Twin-Engined Medium Bomber.

Boost Pressure – Boost is the positive pressure created by a supercharger. It forces more air into the engine to increase its power output. Measured in inches of mercury.

Blue-Nosed Bastards of Bodney – Nickname of the 8th Air Force 352nd Fighter Group who flew P-51 Mustangs out of Bodney in Norfolk, England, in WW2.

Burtonwood – Large USAAF aircraft maintenance base located 2 miles north-west of Warrington, Lancashire, England. It was also known as USAAF station 590.

Chute – American slang for parachute.

Crew Chief – The senior member of the maintenance team who looked after a particular assigned aeroplane. He was usually of sergeant rank or higher.

Cuban and Half Cuban – A vertical aerobatic manoeuvre in the shape of a horizontal figure of eight (Cuban) or half figure of eight (half Cuban).

Donkey – American airman slang for engine.

ETO – WW2 reference to the 'European Theatre of Operations'.

Finger Four Formation – Typical fighter formation for a four-aircraft flight, used by most of the belligerent powers in WW2. When viewed from above, the positions of the four aeroplanes resemble the tips of the four fingers of a human right hand minus the thumb. The middle fingertip represents the flight leader, with the index fingertip on his left representing his wingman. The ring fingertip represents the second element leader and the little fingertip on his right, his wingman.

Fw190 – The Focke Wulf (*Fw*) *190* was a German single-seat, single-engine fighter aircraft designed by Kurt Tank. Widely used by the Luftwaffe during the defence of Germany.

General Ike – General Dwight David 'Ike' Eisenhower. American Supreme Commander of the Allied Expeditionary Force in WW2, Europe. He planned and supervised the invasion of North Africa in Operation Torch in 1942–1943 and the invasion of Normandy from the Western Front in 1944–1945.

Gear – Short for landing gear (the aircraft wheels and their supporting structure). Retracted in flight, lowered for landing.

KIA – Killed in action.

Knot – Measurement of speed – one knot is one nautical mile per hour. NB One knot is roughly equal to 1.15 statute miles per hour.

Maycrete Hut – Prefabricated structure of reinforced concrete posts supporting a pitched roof frame with an infilling of sawdust and concrete panels. Produced by Maycrete Ltd during WW2.

Mags – Short for magnetos, the electrical devices that supply the engine with its ignition sparks.

Messerschmitt 109 – The Me109 was a single-seat, single-engine fighter used by the German Luftwaffe throughout WW2.

MIA – Missing in action.

Nissen Hut – A prefabricated steel structure often used on British and American WW2 military bases. Made from a half-cylindrical skin of corrugated iron.

North American P-51D – A fighter aircraft developed originally for the Royal Air Force, who named it the Mustang after the North American wild horse. After being re-engined with the British Rolls-Royce Merlin engine, it became probably the finest long-range escort fighter of WW2 and was produced in thousands for the USAAF. In its Merlin engine form, it was developed into the P-51B, C and the definitive D model versions (P-51D). They were produced at the Inglewood California and Dallas Texas North American factories. The P-51 of any model was often referred to by both the British and Americans as a 'Mustang'. In our story, we freely use either title.

OC – Officers' Club.

P-47 Thunderbolt – A heavy fighter aircraft used by the 8th Air Force in its early days but mostly replaced by the Mustang in the last twelve months of WW2. Made by the Republic aeroplane company, although successful, it was limited by its relatively short range. Nevertheless, its speed and rugged construction, along with its heavy armament, made it an excellent ground attack fighter. Because of its large and tubby appearance, it earned the nickname of 'Jug'.

Piccadilly Commando – Serviceman's slang name for the ladies of the night who frequented that circus.

Pinks and Greens – USAAF officer's service uniform consisting of a dark green (olive drab shade No. 51) coat worn with trousers of a contrasting colour with a slight pinkish hue. Hence Pinks and Greens.

Quonset Hut – A lightweight prefabricated structure of corrugated galvanised steel, having a semi-cylindrical cross-section. American design based on the British Nissen Hut.

Rolls-Royce Merlin – A 12-cylinder liquid cooled aero engine designed and developed by Rolls-Royce Ltd. Also built under licence in the US by the Packard Company. As fitted to the P-51D in its V-1650-7 form, it could produce 1,490 hp at 3,000 rpm or in its wartime emergency setting 1,720 hp.

RPM – The speed of the propeller measured in revolutions per minute.

S2 Officer – A US Army Air Force intelligence officer.

SNAFU – USAAF serviceman slang term used to express dissatisfaction with one's unit's organisational ability. It stands for (S)ituation (N)ormal (A)ll Fowled (U)p. In reality, a more forceful word than fowled was used!

Split S –To execute a split S, the pilot half rolls his aircraft inverted and executes a descending half-loop, resulting in level flight in the opposite direction at a lower altitude.

T2 – Type of wartime aircraft hangar.

USAAF – United States Army Air Force. Originally known as the United States Army Air Corps (USAAC), it was reconfigured and renamed the USAAF in 1941 and subsequently became the United States Air Force (USAF) in 1947.

The USAAF 8ᵗʰ Air Force – Established as VIII Bomber Command on 19 January 1942, the first units and personnel began to arrive in the UK in late February 1942. It had three major subordinate units: the VIII Bomber Command (BC), the VIII Fighter Command (FC) and the VIII Ground Air Services Command (GASC). Over the next three years, the '*Mighty Eighth*' were expanded to a strength of more than 200,000 people, and at its peak could send more than 2,000 four-engine bombers and 1,000 fighters on a single mission against enemy targets in German-Occupied Europe. It was re-designated as the Eighth Air Force on 22 Feb 1944. In general, the 8ᵗʰ Air Force operated mostly from bases in East Anglia.

The USAAF 8ᵗʰ Air Force Fighter Command (FC) structure in England 1944 – The 8ᵗʰ Fighter Command was made up of three **fighter wings:** the 65ᵗʰ, 66ᵗʰ and 67ᵗʰ fighter wings. Each wing was made up of five to six **fighter groups**. Each fighter group was in turn usually made up of three **squadrons.** At full strength, each **squadron** would be expected to put up sixteen (later in the war, some squadrons could put up twenty-four) aircraft for an escort mission. Each squadron was typically subdivided into four flights, usually known by their colour (red, blue, yellow, etc.). The four aircraft in a flight were numbered, e.g., Red 1 and 2 working as a pair and Red 3 and 4 working as a pair. Red 1 would be the flight leader (of all four) and Red 2 his wingman. Each pair was known as an element, with number 3 being the leader of the second pair and number 4 his wingman.

Yak – A popular propeller-driven Russian training aircraft, often still used today for aerobatic demonstrations throughout the world.

ACKNOWLEDGEMENTS

I would like to acknowledge the help I received from the following people and sources in the writing of this story:

My wife and daughter for their help with the artwork and also for putting up with my constant requests for opinions and advice.

Keith Willington, whom I cannot thank enough, for proof reading and turning my first draft into a readable document.

Anne Smith and Sue Willington and various other friends and family members who were a constant source of encouragement.

The various 8th Air Force books written by the late Roger A. Freeman, a constant and most accurate source of reference.

The Eagle pub in Cambridge, who kindly permitted me to use their establishment in the opening scene of the final chapter.

The internet, especially those websites that have faithfully recorded the accounts of the veterans who were actually there and did it (sadly, most now no longer with us)!

NB The '*Do Not Forget the Defenders*' quote in Kirsten's letter (or similar quotes) is often attributed to Calvin Coolidge, the 30th president of America.

Many thanks to you all.

Richard F. Sugg